THE DARK TERROR

Book Three - The Dark Passage Series

JERRY KNAAK

Published in the United States of America First Printing: 2018

Print

ISBN -13: 978-1-943407-55-2

E-Book

ISBN -13: 978-1-943407-56-9

Trifecta Publishing House

1120 East 6th Street

Port Angeles, Washington

98362

TRIFECTA PUBLISHING HOUSE

Contact Information: Info@TrifectaPublishingHouse.com

Editor: Elizabeth Jewell

Cover Art by Rae Monet

Formatted by Monica Corwin

For Angi

CHAPTER I

I was stunned; I couldn't move. I just stood there, leaning against the wall, chewing on my thumb. What the fuck did I just see? Julie. A vampire baby snatcher? And Sarah. The baby-snatching getaway driver.

Julie was dead, wasn't she? Didn't Detective Dietrich tell me that when he pulled me out of that abandoned coal mine at Land's End? Julie, crucified and murdered out of spite by the vampire who made me, didn't make it. That's what Dietrich had told me. But here she was with my own progeny. The two of them couldn't have looked more maniacal as they made their escape with a freshly hatched newborn.

I had given chase when I saw Julie, but Sarah had screamed out of nowhere and scooped up her compatriot. It was straight out of a movie. Quite the smash-and-grab. They weren't counting on yours truly to spoil the party.

A cloud of smoke and the acrid smell of burnt rubber filled the air as I tried to wrap my head around what had just happened. Headlights and brake lights looked like neon tubes in a time-lapse photo as cars zipped by. Why I was drawn to Alta Bates in Berkeley was crystal clear now. Two nights in a row Julie's vampiric magnetism had attracted me to the area. There was some sort of connection, a psychic bond between me and her. She obviously had been casing the medical center. I didn't know if the bond was because of our lifelong friendship or our kinship as creatures of the night. I didn't make Julie. Allegedly, I'd made Sarah, although I still doubted that. I didn't know how the hell that had happened. My memory lapses had become few and far between, but there were still some gaps, and they were annoying as hell.

The amnesia I'd experienced when I'd first become a vampire made some kind of sense. I was a baby, in essence; I didn't know what was going on, and my body was still adjusting to its new reality. A baby. Now I was chasing vampire baby snatchers. My entire existence had become the truest example of irony ever imagined.

True, I had dispatched a few douchebags since I'd developed the ability to kill with impunity. But I had made the conscious decision not to become some kind of Satanic avenging angel. And now I was faced with a real dilemma. On the one hand, what the hell did I care what Julie and

Sarah did with an infant? I mean, I had a pretty good idea what they were going to do. But seriously, what the fuck did I care? On the other hand, what was left of my human conscience couldn't let them do what they were going to do. I'd never had kids, and I knew kids were out of the question now, but I just couldn't let these two dingbats murder a newborn. I just couldn't. On the third hand, there was a big part of me that wanted to really know what the fuck was going on with them.

This little team-up together happened awfully quick. It had only been a few months since I'd last seen Andrei and Sarah. I knew they had a history; Andrei had admitted as much. Sarah, however, said she was in love with me. Sarah said I turned her. Sarah said a lot of things. And Julie … well … that was the shocking surprise.

The last time I'd seen Julie, she'd died in my arms. Andrei's smug ass and I had duked it out in a battle royal that ended with him at the bottom of a lagoon and me trapped in an abandoned coal mine. Jonas had told me that Andrei was nowhere to be found after the donnybrook at Sutro Baths. Did Jonas know about this turn of events with Julie? He was full of surprises, especially that whole oh, yeah, he's a fucking vampire thing.

My thoughts wandered to Whitney and those memories tugged on my heartstrings like a fiddle player plucking out a tune. That poor girl. I'd really liked her. I saw so much of myself in her, except, you know, the murdering, blood-drinking parts. Since the turning, the nights with Whitney had been the best I'd spent while roaming the streets of San Francisco in the dead of night. As damaged as she was, her artistic abilities and her sensibilities spoke to me. It pained me that I didn't do more to look out for her. It stung that it was Jonas who took her out. That had been one helluva way to find out that my dear detective was a vampire.

It made sense in hindsight. All the clues were there. I never did read him as a prey animal like I had so many others. Hell, I couldn't read him at all. His comfort level with what I was had always been off-putting, considering he empathized with me more than he should have, all the while playing up the detective angle. We were playing each other and didn't know it. My failure to see what he was cost Whitney her life.

And now. Yeah, now. What now?

My inability to protect Whitney weighed heavily on me as I contemplated what to do about Julie and Sarah and the helpless baby they'd spirited off into the night in a red BMW convertible. My experiences with Christina and Sarah were attributable to the fact they had been tainted by vampires, not because I was becoming some weird lesbian vampire.

One of the odd conclusions I had drawn during the time I was this … this … thing, was that we were all a little different. We all brought something different with us to the other side. I was still developing my abilities. I was still trying to understand what I was and what I could be. Survival was the most important thing. Now that I had pretty much figured that out, I supposed the rest would come. Many of the things I was capable of came to me in moments of crisis. Fight-or-flight responses tended to trigger new capabilities. I had spent the past few months refining my powers, learning to control them, and trying to figure out what else I could do.

I had already established that Andrei was a pervert. He had been stalking me since I was twelve, maybe even younger. I had seen him become fog. Lord only knows what other abilities he had. But as far as the two women were concerned, I didn't understand why they were zipping around in a car. Sarah had already demonstrated some shape-shifting ability during our daring *Streets of San Francisco* car chase escape from the cops. Quinn Martin would have been proud.

Maybe because I had overcome my need for such modes of transportation, maybe because my powers were developing at an astronomical rate, maybe because I worked at it … I took BART for the pure pleasure of it, for the want of feeling human once in a while, and I drove when I wanted to be reminded of the tortures of Bay Area traffic. The latter didn't happen very often, but I had developed an affinity for German-made cars, BMWs in particular. So, every once in a while, I boosted one.

So, it was highly doubtful that Julie and Sarah had developed any additional abilities, or they didn't know how to use them. Maybe the personality traits from their mortal lives that were enhanced by the turning weren't helpful to them in their new state. Maybe I was a Russian fighter pilot.

Leaning against a wall and gnawing on my digits wasn't getting me anywhere. And it was certainly not helping the infant that was in imminent danger from a duo of box blonde bloodsuckers.

CHAPTER II

Julie and Sarah had disappeared into the heart of Berkeley in a cloud of exhaust and burnt rubber smoke. A lesser person wouldn't know what to do. A lesser person would have been paralyzed with inaction. A lesser vampire wouldn't know how to pursue her quarry.

I am not a lesser vampire.

I am Elizabeth.

I am Elizabeth Danae Rubis.

And I am the Queen of the Fucking Night.

I took out the pack of cigarettes and a lighter, spun the wheel with my thumb, and put flame to paper and tobacco as I pursed my lips around the filter, all in one smooth motion. Drawing the air and smoke into my lungs as I had taught myself, the tissues inside my dead body burned.

Yeah, I know, I didn't smoke when I was alive, and the nicotine really did nothing for me, but the affectation was a simulation of life that helped me blend in with the mortals. And this moment called for a cigarette.

Tilting my head back and casting my gaze skyward, I forced the smoke from my lungs through my trachea and blew the most beautiful, perfect, round smoke rings. A burning in my eyes and an ache in my brain were followed by the flapping of leathery wings. A squadron of bats appeared overhead. Something *shifted*. I made the mental connection with the lead and saw as she saw. I took gentle control and willed her and her compatriots in the direction Sarah and Julie had headed.

I no longer experienced the headaches or "nosebleeds," or whatever they were. Hours and hours and night after night of practice had mitigated the symptoms of communing with the children of the night. The shift no longer felt forced, it was natural, comfortable even. Critters were still drawn to me. It was a bit unnerving at first, but I'd gotten used to my roommates in short order. And my predatory cat, Blackfoot, didn't hunt them. She didn't exactly cozy up to the spiders and bugs, but she didn't try to eat them either. Birds, on the other hand … let's just say the parrots of Telegraph Hill learned to stay away.

After using my furry, flying friends to find Serge Da Rocha, I was using them to find my best friend and my alleged progeny. Did I really just think that sentence? The colony of bats sensed what I wanted before I wanted it and before I could extinguish my cigarette they were on the girls' trail and in hot pursuit, Anthony Edwards and Tom Cruise be damned.

They left Berkeley and headed east into Oakland along Route 13 and banked southeast along Tunnel Road past Claremont and came to rest in a grove of trees along Lake Temescal. I could see through the eyes of my connection that Sarah and Julie had stopped and parked at the Temescal Beach House. The way they had torn out of Berkeley, I was surprised they hadn't drawn the attention of the local police.

"Well ain't that some shit," I said, as I threw the cigarette down and screwed it into the ground with my booted foot. Now, I could have called the cops. There are a few payphones around, those few that haven't been put on exhibit in museums, and I probably could have found one in short order. I knew Dietrich's pal Tim by name. I'm sure he would have liked to know that there was a vampiric baby-napping ring operating in NorCal. Especially if this crew was connected to his nemesis, Andrei. But I was pretty sure Tim and his SWAT team were no match for two vampires. Hell, they couldn't handle little ol' me.

I scrambled to the top of the building I had been leaning against and took my sprinter's stance. Within three or four steps, I was flapping into the crisp late fall air on my way to Oaktown. The baby-snatching duo wasn't very subtle. They had parked in plain sight in the main driveway of the beach house right off Broadway.

Temescal Beach House was an East Bay Regional Park that featured an actual beach in the middle of the city. I was a bit surprised that they would choose a place near so much water. Temescal was damn near one hundred years old and was a popular spot for events such as weddings. This pricey venue was not what I pictured when I thought of vampiric activities. Dusty, musty old abandoned warehouses, lofts, back alleys, and crypts were more like it.

There could only be one thing at the end of this trail of breadcrumbs, and I intended to find out what the fuck was going on. There was no way an event was going on. It was a bit late, but they couldn't possibly be that brazen, could they?

After transforming back into my "default" state, I surveyed the scene while using the trees as cover. As I took up a position, I watched Sarah and Julie as they sat in the BMW and appeared to be arguing. Hands were gesticulating wildly and heads were snapping back and forth. The car's windows muted their voices, but if body language was any kind of tell, these two were on the verge of an epic cat fight.

I could have used my winged friends for a closer look or listen, but I didn't want to raise suspicions. These new vampires might not have been fully developed, but there was no telling what abilities they could manifest. If my own experience was any indicator, they at least had enhanced senses, especially hearing.

Sarah and Julie finished their argument and appeared to

take simultaneous deep breaths and sigh. Julie reached between the two front bucket seats and scooped up the newborn as if she were the child's mother. Considering what I thought they had in store for the baby, I was shocked at the care and concern. I half expected her to grab the kid by the ankle and drag the infant from the car, and bang its head on the seats, the door frame, and the ground for that matter.

Julie's driver moved with grace and power as she flung the driver's door open. She pivoted in the leather seat and swung her legs out. The soles of her shoes made a solid clap as they hit the pavement of the driveway. Sarah stood straight up, placed her hands on her hips, and arched her back in a stretch as if she had just driven eight hours from San Diego nonstop. After showing no one in particular how limber she was, Sarah surveyed the area. Her eyes narrowed as she cast her reconnaissance in my direction.

I rotated my body behind a large tree with a wide trunk. It wasn't wide enough to conceal all of me, but with the darkness and the shadows, it was enough to keep Sarah from seeing me.

"Would you hurry up?" Julie's shrill, high-pitched voice pierced the night air.

"Would you shut the fuck up? I want to make sure nobody followed us."

"Who the hell would have followed us? We left … her back in Berkeley."

"Yeah, well, something doesn't feel right."

"Yeah, well, *I'm thirsty*."

"Yeah, well, you're the one with the cold feet."

"Look, bitch, I don't know you that well, and this is a baby, for crying out loud. I just don't like this idea."

"Well, bitch, my maker abandoned me, I don't have to answer to her. But I've got nothing better to do, so ... let's do this."

I rolled from behind the tree and took full view of them again. Julie let out an uncomfortable laugh that ended with something that sounded like, "I'm the one waiting on you, bitch ..." or some such. Maybe I imagined that's what she said.

The unlikely couple, and the infant, headed for the main entrance to the pavilion.

Julie led the way, but Sarah sprinted to catch up and pull the door open for Julie so she wouldn't have to try to balance the child awkwardly while she tried to enter the facility. Jules clutched the infant close to her chest as she walked in, and Sarah let the door close behind them as she breezed in.

I stepped forward, reached up and grasped a low-hanging branch with my right hand, and contemplated my next move. Numerous thoughts rolled around in my head as I waited. As I debated what to do, my thoughts wandered. I remembered what I thought I knew about Andrei's modus operandi—identifying victims as adolescents, the method of dispatch. And then there were the traits that manifested after the turning, or the things that were enhanced. I knew how I had been affected, but Dietrich, Andrei, Julie, and

Sarah continued to mystify me. Despite what I knew about myself, I was pretty sure I wasn't done *evolving*. That being the case, what I knew about Andrei was probably only the tip of the fang, as it were.

The baby thing was new … right? I mean, why were Julie and Sarah doing this? Why not attack adults like I had learned to do? I was mortified when I'd killed a child. I'd stayed my hand from killing more. Sarah was my "mistake" or "accident" or whatever. Julie? Well, God only knows how the hell that happened. I was there when she died. Dietrich told me she was dead. But we were all examples of death gone wrong.

Andrei never seemed to want to bond with me. He never seemed to want a relationship. He didn't want to mentor me or teach me the ways of the Force. All that psychic bond bullshit in the vampire movies was just that, bullshit. I never wanted to be close to him, to learn from him, to understand him. I just wanted to kill the fucker, and I thought I had.

Now, I felt like I had to understand him. For some reason, I thought he was behind this, that he was the puppet master pulling the strings. I needed to know why he was using Sarah and Julie to do his dirty work, I needed to know why he was using them to kidnap babies—there was no way this was the first, and I needed to know what the fuck he was going to do with this particular baby. I had a pretty good idea, but I needed to know more.

I hoped I was wrong.

Given Andrei's penchant for pomp and circumstance, I

was in no real hurry. Despite his ability to stand on ceremony, I wasn't one hundred percent sure exactly how he was going to do what he was going to do to this poor child.

Her wail, yes, "her," snapped me out of my contemplative state and spurred me into action. It wasn't close like it should have been. That told me they weren't just on the other side of the door. It was as if the baby cried out from a distance. It wasn't like listening to Sarah and Julie arguing just moments ago - there was space and walls between me and that child. And there was no way in hell I was going to let that stop me. The question was how was I going to do this.

Should I blast through the main doors like Ahhhhnold rescuing Alyssa Milano in *Commando?* Should I go all Black Widow and scramble up to the roof and drop in on the beach side of the building? Should I slink around the side with my back to the outer wall?

Well, there was no way I was going to go bursting into the event space on the other side of the main door without knowing what I was getting myself into. And since I was fairly certain that my quarry wasn't inside the wedding/reception chapel/hall, I decided to employ my recon unit and reconnoiter. The colony of bats left the tree and took flight at almost the exact moment the thought entered my mind.

It didn't take long for me to make the telepathic connection with the lead as the colony banked left over the building toward the lake. Three vamps and a baby were nowhere to be seen. The stone patio was empty except for some outdoor lounge chairs, and the thin strip of beach was deserted.

A one-woman SWAT team I was not, vampire or no vampire. However, Sarah and Julie would be no match for me, but if Andrei was here … let's just say I didn't want to find out. He would be in his element. He was willing his charges to do bad things, very bad things. There was a purpose to this kidnapping. My imagination ran away with the possibilities. All of them ended with a dead baby.

The thought of calling the police popped into my head again. I had done it before. Almost had the bastard too. I was afraid if I did it this time and the Keystone Cops showed up instead of competent police officers, this trio would escape and the baby would be lost forever. It couldn't have been my maternal instincts. I was pretty sure I didn't have any. So, why was I so concerned about this one infant?

Well, there was no way I was going to let Andrei get what he wanted, especially when I knew what that was for once. This demonic love triangle needed to be smashed. Sarah and Julie should not exist, they had no right to exist. A bit hypocritical coming from yours truly, but Andrei had killed Julie to spite me and I'd made Sarah somehow.

This baby didn't deserve what was about to happen to her. That was all there was to it.

I willed a squadron of bats to break off from the main colony and break through the windows—all the windows. And break the windows they did. Simultaneously. It was epic. To the untrained eye, to the uninitiated, it looked like a

Hollywood action movie stunt. A stunt that had taken weeks to coordinate, hours and hours of math, and dozens of pounds of explosives. I used bats. Unfortunately, there were casualties. They could sense my remorse. They bent to my will regardless.

I communed with multiple bats at once and received a three hundred and sixty-degree view of the event hall. What I saw would haunt me the rest of my days.

Sarah and Julie had hold of the baby, one arm each, engaged in a macabre tug-o-war, the infant naked and wailing. Lord only knows when this child last ate; it was probably cold and scared. The element of surprise was mine, and I needed to use it to my full advantage.

Since the main entrance doors opened from the inside out, and I wanted to be as dramatic and intimidating as possible, I directed a group of bats to blow the door outward. This had the effect of heralding my entrance. In all of my Queen of the Fucking Night glory, I blew into the main event hall like a hot dirty vengeful wind.

The combination of my pounding strut and swirling bats gave the impression of a shark slicing through a school of prey fish, only the bats weren't my prey, they were my confederates. My squadron gave way and created a buffer of airspace as I strolled toward this duo of would-be baby killers.

"Beth..." Sarah started. I backhanded her across the room.

"Nobody. Calls. Me. Beth."

Julie rose to her feet, backtracked across the room, and fell into a portable bistro table and water pitcher. I half expected her to go all Wicked Witch of the West and melt when the pitcher dumped its contents on her blonde curls.

"I'm sorry, Elizabeth, I am so sorry."

"I'm the one who owes you an apology for getting you into this mess in the first place, but this isn't the time or the place."

Scanning the room quickly to make sure Sarah and Julie didn't get any bright ideas to outflank me, I approached Julie, who had ended up with the baby clutched in her arms. Sarah was still on the ground with the back of her hand held to her injured mouth. Julie was scared out of her wits. I wasn't worried about either one of them.

I felt confident, powerful ... righteous.

I knew I wasn't going to get the explanation I wanted, at least not now, not tonight. My priority was to abscond with the child and return her to her rightful place. Interrogating Julie and Sarah was not an option right now. But I had the high ground and the fuckers knew it. What surprised me was the absence of Andrei.

That sly grin curled my lips and revealed my fangs. My eyes burned an electric blue I still didn't quite understand.

"I'm taking the baby, Julie."

"Oh, are you now?"

"Yeah, and there's not one goddamn thing you can do to stop me."

"It was her idea!" Julie tossed her head in Sarah's direction.

"Are you fucking kidding me? This was your idea."

"Where's Andrei?!"

"What? Andrei? Why would he be here?" Julie asked.

"You mean to tell me this is all your idea?"

Julie tossed her head in Sarah's direction.

And with that, I directed my winged posse to attack Sarah with impunity. She threw her arms in front of her eyes in an instinctive protective manner, before disappearing in a poof of leathery bat wings and flying off into the night. While she was stunned with the spectacle in front of her, I scooped up the baby from Julie's arms and headed for the exit. Julie made a move to rise to her feet. Her lips were pulled back, her fangs were bared, and she hissed at me. It was a weak hiss; it was more like a leak.

"Julie, don't. Where are the car keys?"

"I-i-i-n the ignition, I think."

"Good answer."

The bats continued to swirl about, and they flew alongside me like a fighter escort as I headed out into the night. My protectors dispersed as I broke the telepathic connection and headed for Sarah's boosted BMW.

CHAPTER III

I searched Sarah's car desperately for something I could swaddle the baby in. I found a sorry excuse for a windbreaker in the sorry excuse for a trunk and wrapped the child in that. I belted her in the passenger seat the best I could. She cooed at me as I looked down at her. Don't even ask me why she felt comforted in my presence. That shit made no sense.

The coupe was responsive to me as I turned it over, threw it in gear, and tromped on the gas. Oh, my, it was like "buttah" as I tore out of the Temescal Beach House parking area and headed for Tunnel Road. Cops be damned, I was getting this kid back to the maternity ward before any angry bitch bats could catch up to us.

I did slam on the brakes once as Tunnel Road turned into Ashby Avenue and I saw California Highway Patrol on the shoulder. The nose of the car dipped as I looked over to see the CHP officer more concerned with paperwork than running radar. It lurched forward again as I mashed the accelerator to the floor.

The eight-minute drive seemed to take an eternity. Throughout all four hundred and eighty seconds I glanced at the rearview mirror frantically looking for a bat that wasn't part of my crew. When I got to Colby Street, I found a parking spot and ditched the car. I exited the vehicle and zipped around to the passenger side and flung the door open. I liberated the baby from the seat belt and scooped her into my arms. She continued to coo. She didn't fuss, she didn't spit up, she didn't whimper. She cooed.

Within seconds we were strutting into Alta Bates like we owned the place. We blew past the emergency room entrance and headed for the main door. A rent-a-cop tried to stand but I shot him a look that froze his blood. *"Don't."* I glared at him and he practically spit up. I looked down at the child. She was a cutie with a full head of dark curly hair —hopefully crib cap would be kind to her—and hazel eyes. As I cradled the child in the crook of my right elbow, I pushed the elevator call button repeatedly. Damn OCD. You can't tell me the elevator doesn't come faster the more you press the button.

The lift finally came. I started to board the car, but we had to wait for twelve people, twelve fucking people—how the fuck did they fit twelve people in here?—to get off. I turned to face the doors as a family of four tried to get on.

"Take the next one." My new vocal range never ceases to amaze me. The look of sheer terror on their faces made me chuckle as the elevator took us to the third floor. I was relieved that no one was waiting for the elevator to take them down when the doors opened. My boots made a distinct sound as I pounded my way to the nurses' station.

"Um, hi, yeah, excuse me, I'd like to return this."

"Um ... ma'am?"

"This baby, I'd like to return it."

Unbeknownst to me, Nurse Ratched over here hit a silent alarm button or some such. Moments later, my acute sense of hearing picked up the distinct sounds of armed security guards or cops galvanized into action and headed in my direction.

"You did not." The nurse peed herself.

I reached over the counter of the nurses' station and grabbed at the alarm-button-pushing bitch, but the fistful of hair I aimed for slipped through my fingers as she pushed backward on her wheeled stool and zoomed away, leaving a trickle of urine behind. Great, another fight-or-flight situation. Oddly enough, I didn't want to do either, I just wanted to return the baby. Despite the jostling, she stayed still and quiet in the crook of my elbow.

As the security guards and cops approached from opposite directions, I turned toward the interior of the space, one hundred and eighty degrees from the way I came. I closed one eye and turned my head away as if I were bracing for impact as I held the baby out in a supplicating gesture.

"Don't move, lady! Freeze!"

As if I was going anywhere.

"I didn't take the baby, I rescued her. And now, I'm returning her."

"Likely story. Hand her over!"

The cop closest to me took the infant from my hands and passed her to a fellow officer.

"On your knees, hands behind your head!"

"Really? That's what we're doing? Do you know how cliché you are?"

"On the ground now! I WILL tase you!"

Now, that was an intriguing possibility. I already knew bullets did little more than put holes in me. Electricity, on the other hand, no clue. Running water, sunlight, churches, crosses, counting, gunshots—these things I knew. High voltage? My mind flashed to the "Escape Clause" episode of *The Twilight Zone,* in which a guy achieved immortality with a deal with the devil and decided to kill his wife just so they'd give him the electric chair, only to be sentenced to life in prison instead. I thought about *The Green Mile* and Doug Hutchison's portrayal of warped Percy Wetmore and the electric chair electrocution gone purposely wrong.

So, yeah, electricity, not so much.

The cop approached me with caution and a pair of less than fashionable bracelets. I thought they might make a kicky belt buckle. He had the chrome-plated cuffs in one hand and the Taser gun in the other. He was going to have to holster one or the other. I chuckled at the thought that it was awful convenient that it was a short walk for me to put the guy in the hospital. The police and hospital security officers continued to slink in my direction.

The wannabe fashion designer officer was finally within striking distance. But I thought better of it. Killing all of these people would be easy. I could open veins and tear out throats with preternatural alacrity while withstanding their weaponry. Then the manhunt, er, womanhunt would really be on. Oh, sure, I become the Good Samaritan and now I get caught. What good would it do me to tear into these armed fools? At best I would get away unscathed. As worst, I'd be riddled with bullets and in custody. But the odds of getting away scot free here were stacked against me. These were beat cops. How soon would my pals from the SWAT team be here?

This standoff needed to end and I had no idea how to end it.

I was thankful that these cops weren't as trigger happy as that SWAT team back at Tunnel Top or the crew at Lands End. Those were the shoot first, ask questions later types. Maybe it was because of the baby, or the fact we were in the maternity ward of a hospital, but these guys were more interested in taking me into custody than shooting the place up and going all Wild Wild West.

"On your knees, NOW!"

"Not gonna happen, chief."

I did place my hands behind my head. I did close my

eyes and wait. But I was damned if I was going to drop to my knees.

Well, that was a lie.

Something *shifted*.

My body collapsed in a heap and all at once I could see a three hundred and sixty-degree panorama. It was like that theater in the round, only, only I was a swarm of … rats? How in the hell? It took several seconds for me to adjust to my new vision. I could see through the eyes of a few dozen rodents all at once, and the effect was disconcerting. My little rat feet skittered across the tile floor in all directions. I saw fur and naked rat tails all about.

The cops, security guards, and nurses yelled and screamed and wailed in horror and disgust. Parts of me had to dodge crushing heel blows and kicks. My pieces disappeared under desks and gurneys and hospital beds, and behind blinking, beeping medical equipment.

This was unlike anything I had experienced to date. All the other shifts involved a singular perspective, except for that night I set out to find Da Rocha; this was frantic and manic and I was literally all over the place. I, we, whatever I was, we probed the space for exit points—air ducts, open doorways, any orifice large enough to accommodate a rat or rats.

We flooded the HVAC system, and I used every ounce of influence I had over my pieces to will us all up. The noise in the aluminum vents was deafening as we made the climb to the rooftop exhaust ports. I'd always wondered what it would really sound like in these vents when I'd watched a movie where the secret agent or burglar infiltrated via the HVAC system. Now I knew. Movies lie. Fuck, this was loud.

I, me, we, the rats converged in one spot on the roof, climbing and clamoring on top of each other and taking on a distinctly human shape. We *congealed*. And I was me again. I looked down at my feet and looked myself up and down, shuddering as I saw a hairless rat tail disappear up my sleeve like a magic trick in reverse.

Confident I was reassembled, I made my way to the edge and looked out over Colby Street. Cops and security guards with guns drawn poured out of the building on to the sidewalk. They would have oozed through the walls if they could have, although I'm not quite sure they knew exactly what they were looking for. Backup units with their flashing lights and ear-piercing sirens were starting to arrive and cordon off the area.

I ran in the opposite direction toward Regent Street. Leaping over voids and more HVAC apparatus, I thought I was home free as I spotted the parapet and prepared to leap into the night sky and fly away.

My foot hit the wall and my leg propelled into open air. Nothing happened. Well, that's a lie. I plummeted to the ground like a rock. What I meant was, no *shift* happened. What was it? Three? Four stories? I landed flat on my face with a dusty thud. I didn't flail. I didn't cry out. I just belly flopped on the sidewalk.

Fuck me.

After a few groans and moans, I muttered, "You have got to be fucking kidding me."

I put my hands alongside me, did a push up, gathered my legs underneath me, and rose to a standing position. Thankfully I didn't land on any parked cars. After dusting myself off and straightening my clothes, I could hear more police vehicles headed in my general direction. It was times like these my enhanced senses came in handy. The sirens were coming from my left, so I broke right and then turned left on Prince Street. Making a right on Bateman, I kicked it into high gear. I made another left, this time on Woolsey, and didn't slow down until I crossed College.

The tree-lined Eton Avenue beckoned, and I took the right fork at Woolsey and Eton. When I got to Claremont, I took a minute. It wasn't that unusual for me to talk to myself. Some of the best conversations I have ever had have been with myself. Usually, I was talking to my cat Blackfoot, but she wasn't around at the moment. So, I paced the corner and tried to reason about what had just happened.

"Goddammit. What the hell?"

Eton dead-ended at a cul-de-sac across the street from where I paced, and I bemoaned my situation. I didn't need any nosy local residents popping out to see what was wrong with the middle-aged lady dressed as a goth. I started walking Claremont headed for Russell Street and Domingo Avenue. When I got there, I parked myself in the middle of a tennis court as far off the road as I could get. I didn't care that it was part of the Claremont country club. I just needed somewhere quiet to sit and think.

Confusion did not begin to describe how I felt about the events of the evening. I don't know what the hell I had expected when I traipsed into Alta Bates with that baby. Of course they'd reacted the way they had. I was probably the last thing they'd seen when Julie absconded with the infant. Granted I'd been chasing her, but she had been a few hundred feet ahead of me, I'd probably obstructed their view, and they thought I'd taken the baby.

Of course, that didn't make any damn sense because I wouldn't have matched the description of the person who took the baby. However, if they hadn't actually seen her … and they saw me running down the street. Ugh. None of that mattered at this point. The baby was safe and back in the hands of the authorities. I wondered how much they'd told the parents. They had to tell them something. I had a feeling they'd leave out the part about the rats.

The scent of chlorine from a nearby pool wafted on the night air and filled my nostrils. Great. A body of water. I shook my head and resumed recounting the night in my head.

What the fuck was going on with Sarah and Julie? It had been pretty obvious from the moment I'd woken up strapped to that giant wooden X that nothing would ever be the same. But what the actual fuck? Julie and Sarah were playing tug-o-war with a baby. I believed in my heart of hearts that they had been about to draw and quarter that child when I'd interrupted them … stop the world, I want to get off. I'd thought they were acting at the behest of Andrei, but I was wrong about that.

I tried to wrap my head around this whole thing.

We were four months removed from dispatching the Billy Badass of all vampire hunters, Jonas was supposedly in Vegas, Andrei was God knows where, and two women who were inexorably connected to me were on the verge of feeding on a baby. Yup. That about summed it up.

Motherfuckers.

CHAPTER IV

For the life of me I could not fathom why Sarah and Julie were hunting newborns instead of adults. But then again, I had killed little Emily and I'd damn near killed that brother and sister. So, maybe the inclination for new vampires is low-hanging fruit. Easy prey. I shuddered at the thought. I hugged my knees and rocked back and forth in the middle of a country club tennis court, trying to formulate theories.

"Why, why, why?"

"Hello, Elizabeth."

A voice out of the darkness. A familiar voice. A comforting voice.

I saw the instantly recognizable silhouette first, and I scooted backward on my ass as it walked toward me.

Jonas.

He was dressed in full film noir detective regalia. Trench coat, gray flannel suit, gangster fedora, filterless Camel dangling from his lip as he lit it with a wooden match.

Bouncing to my feet, I stood up to greet my "friend."

"Cigarette?"

"Please."

He handed me a smoke and lit it for me. I took a long drag that I didn't physically need.

"Where the fuck have you been, Jonas?"

"Vegas."

"How was it?"

"You know what they say, what happens in Vegas ..."

"... stays in Vegas!"

We both laughed out loud and heartily.

"I've missed you, Jonas."

"I've missed you too. What the hell have you gotten yourself into?"

He threw his cigarette on the ground, extinguished it with a well-worn brown leather shoe, and took me in his arms. After a long tight embrace, we stepped back from each other. I wanted to cuss him out about Whitney, but it would keep for now.

"Sarah and Julie have become a real problem, haven't they?"

"How perceptive of you, detective, how very perceptive of you."

"So, the baby isn't obvious to you?"

"No, I just can't figure it."

"You fed on an adult the first time, no?"

"I did, that poor unfortunate orderly in the morgue, or whatever he was."

"Ha. Well, these two newborn vampires are, shall we say, working their way up, building their nerve."

"But what about Andrei? You think he's pulling their strings?"

"Maybe. But doubtful. It's possible that they're useful idiots easily manipulated by a master vampire and still hanging on to their humanity. They can move in and out of decent society without much notice. Andrei, on the other hand, well, let's just say he's not 'natural.' But it doesn't fit who and what he is."

"No shit."

"I've done a fair amount a figuring since I left that night. And I've been back long enough to pick up on what was happening. I figured the girls were doing something like this. I've seen 'junior' vampires feed on the young before."

"Andrei's gotta go, Jonas. Sarah and Julie too."

"No shit. Let's go somewhere we can talk."

"You don't like my tennis court?"

"Ha, no. It's a little too out in the open. This is Berkeley and I know a spot."

"Of course you do."

I popped up and Jonas took my hand in his. Next thing you know, we're crossing streets against lights, dodging what few cars that were out at this time of night, and laughing like a couple of school kids as we dashed through a flash downpour. We burst through the front door of an all-night diner that catered to the college crowd. A bell heralded our arrival.

"Subtle, Jonas."

"Detective Dietrich!"

A portly older woman in archaic waitress garb, interrupted while wiping the counter, beamed when she saw us enter the establishment.

"Who don't you know?" I whispered in his ear.

"Mabel! How's tricks?"

"Everything is fine, fine. Been a long time. Sit, sit. Anywhere is fine."

I surveyed the diner and realized that Jonas, 'Mabel,' a short-order cook in the kitchen, and I were the only people in the joint. We parked ourselves in a booth in the back while Mabel circled around the counter with a pair of water glasses and menus in hand.

"Here you go, kids. Grill's hot, fresh coffee is on. Cuppa Joe?" She regarded us with sparkling blue-gray eyes that peered through a pair of vintage glasses—or were they just old?

I shook my head 'no' while Jonas nodded his 'yes.'

"Okay, then, one coffee for the gumshoe."

Mabel silently delivered Jonas's coffee and gave us plenty of time to peruse the menu.

"How do you know Mabel?"

"Her grandson got into …"

"… a tight spot and you did them a solid."

"Finishing my sentences now?"

"I've seen this movie, I know how it ends. How was Vegas?"

"You asked that already. Um ... interesting? Now's not the time to discuss it. Some other time, perhaps?"

Mabel was back and wanted to know what we wanted to eat. I passed but Jonas ordered "the usual," whatever that was.

"What I really want to know, Jonas, is what the fuck happened that night with Da Rocha? You were the cop, you were the one who was supposed to know what to do in those types of situations."

"Those types of situations don't exist. We committed *murder*. Cops are supposed to uphold the law, not break it."

"Don't give me that self-righteous bullshit. It was self-defense, if you ask me. Da Rocha was going to *end us*, all three of us. Andrei I wouldn't have minded, but I wasn't going to let him kill me, or you for that matter. I may be none too thrilled with what I am, but I am not ready to give in just yet either."

"Well, it won't happen again."

Mabel was back, and this time she had a plate of eggs over easy, hash browns, and toast.

"Here ya go, hon, put it on your tab?"

"Please, and thank you, Mabel."

"Aw, you know as long as I'm here, you never have to worry about the check, detective. Small price to pay for what you done for me and mine."

I just made a face at Jonas that indicated a question that I wasn't going to voice. He knew and he just smiled.

"How can you say it won't happen again, how do you know you won't freeze again if it comes down to it?"

"Well," Jonas said as he shoveled a forkful of egg, runny yoke and all, into his mouth, "because I, like you, understand that Andrei needs to die. And since he's technically dead already, I won't have any trouble offing him. Plus, I have my own reasons. Besides, I stepped up when I had to."

"Yeah, well, took you long enough. How can you eat?"

"Never mind that, that's not important right now."

I ran my fingers through my short cropped hair and grabbed a clump at the crown of my skull and pulled hard. "I just don't understand any of what's been going on. I don't remember turning Sarah, I don't know how Julie turned, I don't know where Andrei squirreled off to after that night with Da Rocha."

"In all my research and studying of case files, Andrei only feeds every so often. I wish I could say there was an exact interval between murders, but there isn't. And yes, the sick bastard identifies his victims at a very young age but never takes them before they 'mature.'" I cringed at that word. "Now, the girls. It's possible he's orchestrating. But my gut tells me they are free agents, doing their own thing and leaning on each other because they don't fully understand what they are."

"That explains a lot. But how do you kill a thing that can become fog?"

"I wish I had all the answers, my dear, but I'm pretty sure we kill him the same way you'd kill either one of us." Hash browns this time, then toast, followed by gulps of coffee. "You transform, do you not?"

"Yeah, well … here's the rub, detective, we all have the same weaknesses. We can't exactly attack him during the daytime, we have to rest. We can't go out in the sunlight when he's most vulnerable."

"Who says?"

"My gut, that's who. I just know stuff."

"Well, unfortunately, your gut is right. We'll have to find a way, Elizabeth, we'll have to."

"How?"

"They'll try for another baby, or a toddler. We'll just have to figure out where they're going to strike next, or get ahead of them and figure out where they rest during the day. As for Andrei …"

"Why doesn't he just hunt on the regular like me?"

"Like you? Nobody hunts like you. Because he knows it's not safe, he knows that's what gets him on the radar. That's why he was so upset with your drawing so much attention to your … exploits. It was drawing unwanted attention."

"Well. there was that one time that I called you guys. Well, Billy called you. I just told him what to say."

"That was you? I wondered where that tip came from … and speaking of …"

"The fucker betrayed me."

"Elizab …"

"Shut it, I don't want to talk about it."

"But his whole fam …"

"I warned him."

"Eliza …"

He reached for my hand, and there was a time I would have let him, but not now.

"*Shut it,* Jonas. Seriously. I really don't feel like I have to explain myself to you, or anyone else for that matter. Especially *you*. I didn't ask for this. And you know damn well what I am, what *we* are. So, you don't get to lecture me about my eating habits, or my bloody revenge habits, especially after what you did to Whitney. If it was up to you, Serge Da Rocha would still be trying to end us. And yeah, what I still don't get, why the fuck didn't you pull your service weapon? Why did we have to go all *Kung Fu Fighting* on the beach?"

"Oh, we're back to this. If you must know, and I am sure you know already, I had to turn in my weapon and my badge."

"Oh, you don't have a backup piece?"

"You watch too many cop shows."

"Don't bullshit me."

"Well, you supposedly finished Andrei."

"Don't, just don't. That's false equivalency, Jonas, and you know it."

"You've changed. It's been what, six months?"

"Damn Skippy I've changed. I'm not some babe in the woods anymore. I've learned a lot, I've done a lot … hunted and killed a lot."

I looked away as the last three words trailed out of my mouth and dribbled down my chest. Shame wasn't the right word. Killing was a necessity. Killing was part of my existence. Killing was fun ... sometimes. I don't know why I was being sheepish about it. I felt like a teenager who had just copped to smoking weed. Subsisting on small woodland creatures didn't cut it.

"But you still have a lot to learn, Elizabeth. You're too impulsive, too high profile, too ... out in the open."

"Now you sound like him."

"That's not my intention. You said not to lecture you, and I won't. But we have some harsh realities to deal with here. Your best friend and your one-night stand are quite possibly aiding and abetting your maker in infanticide. That's a real problem, and we need to deal with it."

"You better not be a pussy this time."

"I won't."

"Because there's nothing worse than a pussy vampire. Especially an ex-cop pussy vampire."

"Ha ha, very funny, Miss Rubis."

With that we shared a good-natured, honest-to-goodness chuckle, and some measure of reassuring warmth returned between us. I was still skeptical of Jonas's fighting skills. His detecting skills were never in question, but I needed to know I could count on him in a scrap.

"I won't let you down this time, Elizabeth, I promise."

"Good, because we've seen this fool turn into fog; God

only knows what else he can do. Sarah can already transform into a bat."

"How do you know that?"

"I've seen it."

"Oh." After a long pause, and some staring into space, he said, "It's getting late ... er ... early, depending on your perspective. We should get you to your resting place. Ready?"

"Not so fast, Columbo. I'm not ready for you to know where that is just yet. I can manage."

"Meet back here tomorrow night?"

"Sure."

I'm not ready for *you* to know where my spot is, either.

CHAPTER V

It was time to update my look again, and I was pretty sure I needed a professional. Cutting and coloring my hair without the benefit of a reflection in a mirror had me looking a mess. Sarah's wardrobe was on point, and I found more items that fit than not. Jonas would have told me if I had blood stains on my face or dried blood down the front of me. Wouldn't he?

A good cut and color were in order. But I couldn't just stroll into Supercuts. I was going to have to find a salon that was just about to close for the night with a solo stylist. So many shops, so many choices. I couldn't make up my mind if I should hit one of the chains—Supercuts, Great Clips, Sport Clips—or should I find an independent shop? There were plenty of both.

What I really needed was a spa day, or a spa all to

myself. Where were Saul Goodman and his salon office when I needed them? A good sauna session, a facial, a mud bath, and a massage, plus hair and a mani/pedi, and I'd be good to go.

As much as I knew I could hypnotize a stylist, I didn't think I could mesmerize the staff of a day spa. I didn't rule it out. It just wasn't in the cards for right now.

An independent shop with minimal staff was the wiser choice. Before long, I found a salon in Berkeley that was just about to close. The stylist, a well-appointed mature woman in her mid-fifties who was just about to flip the sign from "OPEN" to "CLOSED" and lock up for the night, found me towering over her.

"Hi."

"We're … um … closed?"

"Oh, honey, I think you've got time for one more customer for the night."

My eyes locked on to hers. My eyelids widened and my glare burned into her brain. Her eyelids widened to match mine, her pupils dilated, and she slipped into my control. Without saying a word I willed her to open the door and go back inside. Once in the salon, I flipped the sign to "CLOSED" and locked the deadbolt.

Mechanically, robotically, she began to prepare her workstation for me.

"Have a seat," she deadpanned.

After I took my place in the chair, she wrapped the smock around me and fastened it at the back of my neck. It was disconcerting looking in that mirror and not seeing me in it.

"What's your name?"

"Mary. And what are we doing today?"

"Well, Mary, let's trim this mess and color it while we're at it. I'd like to go back to my natural brunette."

"Let's wash it first."

Mary led me to the back where the sinks were. I sat in a recliner, tilted my head back, and let Mary gently wash my hair. The warm water and shampoo infiltrated the short strands and soaked through to my scalp. I allowed myself to relax and enjoy Mary's fingers in my hair washing away days and weeks of grime and muck. She took it upon herself to wash my face, neck, and ears.

I was getting thirsty.

Mary sat me up, toweled me off, and led me back to her workstation. Mechanically, robotically, methodically, Mary prepped my hair and applied the color. I patiently waited the thirty minutes while the color set. I stared at her certificate from cosmetology school. After rinsing, I sat back in the chair.

"How would you like it cut and styled?"

Mary ran her fingers through my hair and stared into the mirror as if she could see me, as if I were a normal, regular customer.

"Just trim it up and make it nice and neat. Think pixie."

I couldn't believe the words that were coming out of my mouth. "Pixie?" Who the hell was I? Elizabeth Danae

Rubis, Greek Goddess with the long curly tresses, chopped and thrice-colored, was asking for a pixie cut? It could be worse, I guess. I could be dead and buried. If I was going to mix and mingle and blend in, I was going to need to look presentable. I could shower regularly and boost a new wardrobe as I went along, but my hair was a long neglected story. I had chopped it and colored it to go incognito. And now I wanted to look good again?

My look from the neck down was quite pleasing. I was happy with the ensemble I'd put together from Sarah's closet. It was a look I absolutely rocked. The boots … I did have to replace the coat after the hawk in the park … but the "Legend of Billie Jean" haircut didn't suit me at all. Despite being undead, I couldn't imagine being pale, with white pasty skin like Bela Lugosi. What skin I could see was still as olive as it had been when I was alive. There was an iridescence to it, a pale sheen, but the color was as normal as it ever was.

Mary deftly, albeit mechanically, robotically, methodically, worked the scissors and clippers through my hair. I closed my eyes and imagined what it would be like to see what she saw. Unlike my communal abilities with creatures of the night, I could not achieve such a connection with Mary. I tried.

"How's that?" Mary obviously had no idea that I cast no reflection in the mirror and therefore could not inspect her handiwork that way. "Um … what do you think?"

"Much better."

Did I mention I was getting thirsty?

From what I could see on the smock and the floor, Mary hadn't taken much off. But there were locks and strands and clumps that indicated that she did *something*. She absent-mindedly stroked my head and my hair as if I were a normal, regular customer. I let my mind wander, hoping to find a critter to channel—a rat, a mouse, a spider even; but I found nothing. I had to trust Mary and her assessment.

She squirted some mousse into her hand and rubbed her hands together before applying it to my hair. She then combed and brushed my locks carefully, meticulously. After blow-drying my hair, and using the device to blow the loose hair off of me, Mary removed the smock and folded it over her arm. I stood up and turned on a heel to face her. I locked eyes with her again, and this time I didn't let go.

I moved toward Mary methodically, robotically, deliberately. She backed away and blinked. My hypnotic hold over her loosened. She blinked, swallowed hard, and said dreamily, "We're closed."

"Oh, no, my dear, you are definitely … open."

I grabbed her upper arms and brought my face to her chest. Her heartbeat quickened; her heart threatened to thump right out of her chest as I inhaled her from her sternum to her nose.

"What are you do …?"

"Shhhhh."

With my left hand, I grabbed her chin and tilted her head to my left. My lips were so close to her neck I could feel the tops of the goose bumps as they formed. What a delicious sensation. Her jugular vein throbbed through the gooseflesh and begged for my fangs. I did not make that vein wait long.

Mary's scream become a moan in short order as the point of my razor-sharp fangs pierced her skin and opened her jugular. The life-giving blood poured into my mouth, and the initial metallic taste gave way to a sweetness tinged with sadness. I sucked at her neck and took her to the floor as she weakened. The dark liquid flowed steadily as I took in every last bit of it. Mary faded away as her heart thumped for the last time. A long line of blood was strung from the wound in her throat to my mouth and stretched as I stood up and lorded it over Mary.

I wrapped the blood string around an index finger, snapped it with a yank, and sucked the sweet nectar off my digit with a slurp. After dragging my stylist to the broom closet and stuffing her in among the mops and cleaning supplies, I closed the door, turned on a heel, and headed for the exit. Time to meet Jonas. I wondered if he would like my hair. Guess we were about to find out. I was going to be late, and I frankly didn't give a fuck.

CHAPTER VI

I breezed into the diner like I owned the joint, never mind Jonas and his waitress pal. Air of ownership of establishments was getting to be a habit. Jonas was in the back booth, and Mabel was doing Mabel things— wiping the counter, refilling coffee cups, joking with the patrons, restocking the napkin and condiment dispensers. She glanced up when the bell above the door jangled my arrival and nodded in Jonas's general direction. A genuine, warm smile curled her thin lips. She was immaculately appointed in her 1950's waitress garb. I thought I had stepped through a wormhole.

There was Jonas, in his gray flannel suit and trench coat, pinching the top of his fedora with one hand and stirring his coffee with a spoon in the other. I wouldn't have been surprised if my vision had shifted to black and white as someone shoved the muzzle of a heater into my lower back. But Sam Spade was nowhere to be found.

I sauntered over to Jonas's table and stood there staring at him until he acknowledged me. When he looked up after what seemed like an eternity, I said, "You're in my seat."

"Oh, am I?"

I didn't like having my back to open spaces, especially open spaces that contained people, people I didn't know. I liked being able to keep my eye on the door and watch the comings and goings. I had been taken by surprise too many times, and I was determined to minimize that risk.

Jonas rose to his feet and stepped out of the booth. He arched his back to avoid making contact as he realized I wasn't going to move. After he slid into his new seat, I slipped into the one he had just vacated. As he looped his index finger around the handle of the coffee mug and slid it across the table, he looked up at me. His elevator eyes didn't stop at the same floor as mine. They went to the top floor.

"I like your hair. Do I want to know ..."

"No, you don't."

"Okay, then."

"I wanted to go back to my natural color. The platinum blonde was too much of a contrast with my Mediterranean complexion."

"I hate to tell you this ..."

"Shut it, Jonas."

"So, are you going to tell me where your new hideout is?"

"Nope. 'Hideout?' Are we in a Hardy Boys novel?"

Jonas didn't answer; he just sipped his coffee.

"How can you?"

"You learn."

"What does your body do with it? I mean ... it's not blood."

"Well, I throw it up eventually. The trick is being able to keep it down long enough to keep up the ruse. That's what takes practice, that's what you have to learn. And I like the affectation."

"The thought of human food or drink makes my stomach churn. I don't know if I could."

"'Human?' Listen to you. A vampire for six months and you're talking like you're a different species."

I leaned across the table, got in Jonas's face, and hissed, "Well, we are, aren't we?"

"That's just it. I don't know."

"What do you mean, you don't know? You're what, one hundred years old?"

"More like ninety, but whatever. Look, I've managed to develop a few ... techniques over the years."

"You know what, Jonas, one of these days, you're going to spill it. You're going to tell me everything ... from the beginning."

"Well, you already ..."

"All. Of. It. From the beginning. But today is not that day. What I know right now is that Andrei needs to go. The baby's blood I get. You'd think they'd find something easier than a smash and grab in a hospital. As for Andrei, I have this sinking feeling he never left the Bay, and he's running those two."

"That still doesn't makes sense. I think you're onto something, though. Maybe not with the baby thing, but he could be mentoring them. But to what end, I wonder."

"Control. To do his bidding. They aren't his type; they don't fit his MO. But he has two disciples, whether he really wanted them or not. Julie I don't get yet, but Sarah is very impressionable. She gets attached way too easily."

"And you know this how?"

"That's not important right now, just trust me, I know."

Mabel came by to refill Jonas's coffee mug with what looked like motor oil with a few hundred thousand miles on it. She gave me a look as if she wanted to get me something, and I shooed her away with a quick shake of my head. As her eclipse of my view passed, I realized that the three of us were the only folks left in the front of the joint, and that just left the short-order cook in the kitchen.

"I don't think your hair is going to grow back."

"Thanks for that, Jonas. I kinda figured that already. I thought about that going in when I chopped it all off. Survival was more important than vanity at the time. What's the matter, Jonas, you don't find me that alluring; you're not attracted to me?"

My tone shifted from irritated to playful in the matter of a sentence, and Jonas didn't quite know what to think or say.

The look on his face spoke volumes as he tried to figure it out.

"Of course I find you … ahem … um … attractive, it's just that …"

"What, Jonas?"

I lowered my voice an octave, bit my bottom lip, and put on my best smolder.

He cleared his throat, hard.

"It's just that I think we should … um … stick to the task at hand. What to do with Andrei, how to, you know."

I traced the veins on the back of Jonas's hand with my index finger, flirtatious, teasing. After allowing it for a long moment, Jonas yanked his hand back and glared at me. I found myself enjoying him, enjoying his company, forgetting his failure during the fight with Da Rocha, wanting him, needing him. There was something about him. Boyish charm. His old-fashioned nature.

"I have some news."

Those four words broke the spell. I'd fully intended to seduce Detective Dietrich, but his deadpanned, "I have some news," snapped me back to reality.

"Way to ruin a mood and a moment, Jonas."

"Yeah, sorry. It's just that … well …"

"Out with it. For fuck's sake, spill it!"

"Your brothers are back in town."

Fuck me sideways. That's all I needed right now was a familial complication.

"Goddammit, Jonas! Next time, say that, start with that. Don't let me get all into ..."

"Wait, what? You're into ..."

"That's not important now, is it? What the hell, Jonas? How did you find out? Never mind, I don't need to know. Any idea why they're here? I figured they would've dealt with the estate by now."

"That's just it. They can't if you're still alive."

"But I'm not. There was a thing, a memorial, or whatever. I was declared dead. You were there, for crying out loud."

Mabel dropped a coffee cup. The sound of shattering porcelain made us stop our bantering and give her the side eye.

"Sorry, kids. You go back to whatever it is you're doing."

I dropped my voice to a whisper while Mabel got out a whisk broom and a dustpan and swept up the pieces of the broken mug.

"Look, Jonas, as far as the world is concerned, I'm fucking dead. D-e-d, dead."

"It's not that simple. No body, no death, regardless of what the coroner had to say about it. We all saw them pronounce you dead, or saw you on the slab. But the fact of the matter is a morgue attendant was bled dry and your 'body' vanished without a trace, technically."

"Fuck that. I do not want to be the reason my brothers don't get what's coming to them, or to keep them from handling Mom and Dad's affairs, considering I'm the one who caused this in the first place."

"They've been asking a lot of questions, poking around. Openly questioning if you are really dead."

"This isn't the fourteenth century. Bodies don't just get up and walk off."

"You did."

"Yeah, well … still. Body snatcher, grave robber, clerical error. All logical, plausible explanations."

"Look, you're going to have to deal with it at some point. They are knocking on a lot of doors and asking a lot of questions."

"Tell me again how you know all this?"

"I spoke with Tim."

"Oh, fuck me. This just keeps getting better by the minute. You should learn to lead with the distressing shit instead of getting all warm and cozy and lulling people into a false sense of whatever the hell. Tim has been trying to put me in the ground since Jump Street."

"I didn't tell him anything. He already knows you're upright and walking around. He doesn't know how or why. I thought maybe he'd be able to give me a line on Andrei. Some kind of tip as to where I could find the bastard."

I don't know why, but I suddenly became aware that Jonas and I were the only two souls left in the diner. The kitchen was quiet, and Mabel was nowhere to be seen. Just then, the big plate-glass front picture window of the diner imploded. A deafening blast was followed by flying shards of broken glass daggers. Instinct spurred Dietrich into action as he dived across the table and grabbed me. He threw his body between me and the concussion of the next blast that removed the rest of the windows from the frames. Tear gas canisters flew through the spaces where the windows used to be and hit the tile floor with a metallic "thunk" as they emptied their foul green contents into the air around us.

Within seconds, familiar sights and sounds filled the atmosphere. SWAT team sounds, cop sounds, militarized police sounds, laser sights, assault rifle fire.

"Goddammit, Jonas, you didn't think for one moment that meeting with Tim would be a *bad* idea?"

I shouted this at him while we were on the floor underneath the table where we had just been conversing and plotting and flirting. Now that table was the one thing keeping us from being perforated. Unfortunately, the next move wasn't readily apparent. As much as I insisted on sitting where I could see everything, I hadn't bothered to case the joint for exits or emergency egress points. Then again, I hadn't thought Jonas would do something this stupid.

"It's a good thing I didn't tell you where my hideout was. Shit, Jonas, you would have led these assholes right to me. And how do I know you're not working with them?"

"Um, hello, they're shooting at me too!"

"Hello! Like that matters when we are what we are. I've been shot more than a few times. You'd hardly know it if you saw me naked, which at this rate you never will, unless you figure out a way to get us the fuck out of here."

"Oh. Um. Okay, okay. Give me a minute, I need to think."

I wasn't sure if he was trying to think of a way to escape or if he was imagining me naked. Probably both. Typical.

"We don't have a minute, Jonas, so you better think of something, and fast."

The laser sights were growing in number as they swept back and forth searching for their quarry. The heavy jack-booted footsteps got louder and louder. These guys were not subtle, that's for sure. I really didn't want to have to go hand-to-hand with these guys. I preferred to find a way out that didn't involve slaughtering a SWAT team.

Over the past six months I'd often wondered why the dragnet hadn't closed around me. Why hadn't the authorities found me sooner? I wasn't subtle about my feeding habits. I'd left quite the bloody wake behind me. I'd had a few encounters with the SFPD's militarized unit and always managed to escape. Dietrich's buddy Tim must have either followed him or put some kind of tracking device on him. My guess was the latter. Why Tim didn't haul Jonas's ass in based on what had happened at Local Edition I'll never know. Hopefully, I'd get a chance to ask Dietrich.

Right now, my only concern was getting the hell out of here without any new bullet holes.

When the shooting stopped, I could hear the telltale sounds of SWAT uniforms and equipment. The crackle of radios and sounds of armored limbs crept closer and closer as the points of the laser sights danced on the opposite wall and through the window into the kitchen. The laser light show would have given a cat an epileptic seizure. An image of Blackfoot flashed through my brain. I thought of all the times she simply showed up out of nowhere and seemed to disappear into thin air. That cat had found me in the strangest places and entered areas you'd think were impossible to access.

I closed my eyes and took a deep breath I didn't need. Something *shifted*.

POOF

Poof is the only word that describes what happened. One second I was crouched down under a table, and the next I was filling up the space as I searched for an exit. Jonas was going to have to fend for himself. I could see in a full three hundred and sixty degrees, once again. You'd think I had just transformed into a horde of rats, but you'd be wrong. Smoke? Fog? I was nowhere and everywhere. I was mist. It took a moment or two, but my thoughts coalesced, and I tried hard to focus.

I channeled my inner Blackfoot, thought about how she might get out of a place like this, and willed my swirling, gaseous form under the restroom door. It wasn't exactly catlike, but it was the best thing I could come up with. Concentrating with all my might, I tried to flip the wall switch, the switch that controlled the fan. On the third or fourth try, the switch gave in. The light and fan hummed to life at the same time, and within seconds the restroom was filled with an Elizabeth mist tornado. My disembodied form swirled and twisted as I was sucked into the restaurant's HVAC system.

The chimney spewed me out into the cold night air. Twisting and turning above the diner, I watched as the SWAT team, still wearing their gas masks, stormed the building. I hovered for just a moment, trying to catch a glimpse of Jonas, before willing myself down along the ground. Before long I was a moisture-filled wisp accelerating south along Route 24. Horns blared and high beams switched on as I weaved between cars and created near whiteout conditions for the hapless drivers. I headed west at I-580, narrowly avoided getting sucked into the ventilation system of a tractor trailer, and wrapped myself like Christmas garland around the main spire of the new east span of the Bay Bridge. It reminded me of the Sunshine Skyway Bridge from that one time I'd visited Tampa for a public relations conference. It was too bright.

After forcing a transformation back into "human" form, I crouched at the top of the spire and got the lay of the land. Traffic on the bridge was heavy for this time of night. Bright headlights leading the cars pierced the darkness and lit up the roadway. I got to sixty-four when I realized I was counting the cars. Shaking the cobwebs loose from the absentminded counting spell took a self-inflicted slap to the face. I was dizzy like King Kong hanging on to the Empire State building for dear life as the biplanes swooped in for the kill. The lights and the counting disoriented me.

That's when I noticed the helicopters—news and police.

There was no way I was going to let them find me at the top of this spire. My form may have been silhouetted against the black sky, but that would be no defense against searchlights. I needed to move and fast. I closed my eyes and steadied myself. The wind buffeted me and my clothing as I swan dived off the spire. I used almost all of the five hundred and twenty-six feet to transform into bat form. Spray from the Bay hit me in the face as my wing tips dipped into the tops of the waves. Flapping those wings as hard as I could, I gained altitude after finding an updraft. It took just fifteen minutes for me to reach my sanctuary.

And no, you do not get to know where it is … yet.

CHAPTER VII

W hat I will tell you is that I was extremely distressed when I arose the next night. Just when I thought I could trust Jonas things went sideways … again. How could he be so careless? He'd met with Tim and next thing you know, the SWAT team was on us. Either he was followed or he was tracked electronically somehow. He wasn't careless enough to be followed. Jonas would have made sure of that, especially when he was meeting with me. He wouldn't have put me in that kind of danger. What was it then? A bug? A GPS tracker? Cell phone triangulation? Did Jonas allow Tim to touch him in any way when they saw each other? A handshake, a bro hug?

And what the fuck was Jonas talking about when he said my brothers were back in town? What the hell did they want? Too bad the SWAT team had interrupted our conversation. I needed Jonas for more than one reason. He was going to have to help me take down Andrei. There was no way I could handle Andrei and his two concubines by myself. And he was going to have to help me with this familial situation.

My brothers.

The only people who had believed me when I tried to tell everyone someone had been in my bedroom all those years ago. They teased me mercilessly when we were children, their little "Beth."

"Come on, Beth, fight back! Come on, Beth, what are you going to do about it? Daddy's little girl, come on, Beth, are you going to tell Daddy?"

"Stop it, stop it, STOP IT!"

But if anyone outside the family gave me grief, they were ready to scrap at a moment's notice. More than one would-be suitor found that out the hard way. And bullies? Oh, boy, I'd almost felt sorry for one boy who'd pulled my pigtails and pushed me around. My brothers had beat him within an inch of his life.

"Nobody fucks with our sister!" They taunted, "Except us, that is." I could hear their laughter echoing down the hallway. "That's what you get," I said under my breath as Julie put her arms around me and led me away. We were what, nine? Nobody bullied me in school ever again.

But at home, I was their little "Beth." My poor Barbies were kidnapped and tormented by a platoon of GI Joes.

Heads shaved and conscripted into a make-believe army, their limbs were blown off by firecrackers and bottle rockets. My bedroom became a M*A*S*H unit as I tried to piece the plastic back together time after time.

That had all changed when I was twelve, and I'd started seeing the face in the window. That had all changed when Andrei broke into our house and started touching me in my sleep. Night terrors, they called it. Overactive imagination, they said. OCD, ADHD, an alphabet soup of medical terms were hurled at our family. The only problem was, I was an exemplary student. No discipline issues. No attention-span problems. If I got bored with a subject it was because I couldn't stand waiting for the rest of the class to catch up. Not because I had some neurological disorder that needed to be medicated.

Nobody believed me.

Psychiatrists. Psychologists. School nurse. Guidance counselors. Teachers. My parents. Nobody. Nobody except my idiot brothers. Paolo and Stavros were my only allies. Every time I awoke in a panic, drenched in sweat, they were ready to fight. They would burst into my room armed with whatever they could find—tennis rackets, golf clubs, baseball bats, whatever. That night Andrei had cut my foot, Paolo and Stavros swore they saw the bastard … in the window and then outside running across the front lawn. Nobody believed them either.

Julie listened all right. She'd let me cry on her shoulder. She'd held me when I needed it. But she didn't believe me.

Not in a real way. In more of a "there-there" kind of way. She fucking believed me now, didn't she?

I did not need Paolo and Stavros here now. How could they or anyone else think I was still alive? Everything in the wake of my parents' deaths should have been handled by now. There must be probate issues. Was my missing body the holdup? Wasn't there a policy or a procedure or something in the event of a missing corpse? I had been pronounced dead, for fuck's sake. I had been there. There had to be a death certificate. The last thing I wanted to do was prevent my brothers from claiming their inheritance. This was going to bother me. My brothers were a lot of things, but above all else, they were family men, and they deserved what they had coming to them. Their crazy-ass vampire sister shouldn't stand in the way of that.

I was going to have to deal with that and them eventually. But before then, I needed to find out what was happening with Jonas. Did he survive the SWAT team attack? If he did, where was he? Did he get away? Was he arrested? I felt shitty for what I'd done to get away, but I hadn't known what else to do. I'd acted on instinct. Knowing what Dietrich was, I'd figured he would do the same. However, I didn't know what his capabilities were. All I knew was that he was like me in that he needed human blood to survive. That's why he'd taken Whitney. I thought maybe he could float in the air based on Whitney's drawing. Beyond that, I didn't know what he could do.

My abilities, on the other hand, seemed to be evolving.

Dietrich could float, Andrei could become fog, but Elizabeth Danae Rubis, well, let me tell you ... rats, a bat, and mist, and seemingly at will. Plus my command of the children of the night. Yeah. Fight or flight spurred my transformations. I had mastered the shift to bat. I could pretty much manage that whenever I felt like it. But those last two—mist and rats—those were new.

The hypnotic abilities were the first that I had realized. The voice, the stare. I could will almost anyone to do my bidding. My voice affected people in ways I didn't understand. That had been evident with Julie at the abandoned house at Moss Beach. And at Anthropologie. And with the Willy Loman mess of a man. The waitstaff when I was hanging out with Whitney.

But the physical transformations. The communing with the creatures, the children of the night. As much as I used these elements to my advantage, I was still mystified by the how and the why. What was I, really? Was I so different from Sarah, Julie, Jonas ... Andrei? What made me so special? Was I?

After that night with Andrei when I was twelve, my brothers hadn't teased me so much. They were kinder, gentler, more protective. And if they knew what I had done to our parents, what their little "Beth" had done ... I might not be long for this world. There was no way I could let them find out. And nobody calls me "Beth."

CHAPTER VIII

As much as I was enjoying the trip down memory lane, Jonas Dietrich was my priority. I would deal with my brothers after I found Jonas.

There were only a few possibilities.

He'd been aerated by a hail of bullets and existed no more. I found that one hard to believe. I had been shot, more than once, and I survived. Jonas was older and more powerful. Vampire Anatomy 101 would indicate that we could withstand the worst these militarized cops would dish out with conventional weapons.

He'd escaped as I did. He'd found a way out of the main dining area and shimmied through a crack or a hole. He'd transformed into a critter or critters of some kind and found a crevice to hide in or scoot through to safety. I wasn't sure of Jonas's abilities. But if I could become a bat, mist, a horde of rats, if I could commune with the children of the night, what could Jonas do?

Or he'd been arrested. Rather than reveal his true nature, he'd simply given in and allowed his old mates to take him into custody. This theory didn't make any damn sense. What would he do about his sunlight allergy? He would have to be "awake" during the daytime. Folklore said we needed to rest in the earth we were buried in. I was the exception to the rule because I had never been interred. That was my story anyway, and I was sticking to it. What would happen to Jonas if he wasn't allowed to return to his resting place by cock crow? Did I just really think, "cock crow?"

"What do you think, you little skank?" I asked Blackfoot. She had climbed into my lap after I awoke from my daytime slumber. She mewed and purred as I scratched her between the ears. "What do you think happened to our dear policeman, you mangy feline, hmmm?"

And what about Blanche or Gert or Mabel, whatever the fuck her name was? Was she tipped off somehow? Did she rat us out? I found it hard to believe that one of Dietrich's beneficiaries would have turned him in. But then again, look at how Billy did me. I never expected that to happen either. And we know how that turned out.

I was tempted to summon my best reconnaissance pals and send them out into the night to try to find the good detective. But I had a sinking feeling that it was the third scenario that had actually played out. The realist in me imagined Dietrich surrounded by the SWAT team and refusing to harm them. Unlike yours truly, who had no problem opening a few arteries at Tunnel Top. He didn't seem to want to acknowledge what he was. So I highly doubted that he'd sprouted wings and flown away in the face of all that firepower.

If Jonas had been arrested at that spot, where would he have been taken? And how did SFPD have jurisdiction? Some kind of interdepartmental cooperation thing, I imagined. So, he had to be in San Francisco. I was starting to suspect that his boy Tim knew what we were, or at least what Jonas was. Precautions had to be taken, concessions made to keep Jonas "alive" so they could interrogate and incarcerate him. But to what end? To find me? Andrei? His two bimbo concubines? Any and all vampires in the area?

As usual, I had more questions than answers.

Well, it was time get some fucking answers, goddammit.

I thought about what Jonas would do in this instance and went back to the diner. I wasn't sure what I would find, but I was hoping that some clues to Jonas's fate had been left behind. These cops weren't exactly what you'd call "subtle." They seemed to have murderous intent in their hearts rather than justice, if my encounters with them were any indication. But if Tim knew what Jonas was, or what we were, he had to know shooting at us wasn't the answer. Maybe he thought all that firepower would slow us down or incapacitate. Serge Da Rocha had had a better chance of stopping us, and he was dead.

My fight-or-flight responses were remarkable, and I was stunned that Jonas didn't employ the same when faced with dire circumstances. But then again, I didn't do these things on purpose, they just *happened*. Why didn't they just *happen* to Jonas? Maybe they did. Maybe I just wasn't around to see it.

The diner was a shambles. Yellow crime scene police tape was strewn about the place. Windows were left in shards on the ground. Shell casings were littered all over the sidewalk and were marked with those little evidence flags. These cops must've thought they were righteous in their cause, because they sure as hell didn't take care to clean up their mess or hide their intentions. You'd have thought this had been a gangland shootout. You'd be wrong.

A couple of members of the kitchen staff were the only people about the place, and they were doing their best to straighten up. Racist and prejudicial of me, I know, but at first glance, I didn't think they spoke much English. They were cleaning the kitchen, mopping and sweeping and tidying up. You'd have thought they were getting ready to open for the late evening crowd. You'd be wrong.

"¿Donde estan Señora de la casa?" My Spanish was limited and I knew I'd butchered the question. But they knew what I meant. "En su apartamento." "¿Cuál es la dirección? Escríbelo." The more scruffy of the two, the burly, dirty one, wrote Mabel's address down on the order pad and tore it off like he was putting in an order for bacon, eggs, and toast. He handed it to me grudgingly as he looked me up and down with disdain. "Puta," he spat at me. I flew to him, I *flew*, and grabbed him by the grungy collar of his ratty grease-stained t-shirt. Pressing him against the grill, I bared my fangs and hissed. "Not puto … vampiro."

His skull made a sickening cracking sound as I took his face in my hands and smashed his head against the wall over and over and over and over again. "Call me puta, eh?" His coworker slipped and fell as he tried to turn and run. He skittered across the floor on all fours as he tried to scramble to his feet. His eyes widened and his jaw dropped as I closed in on him. His neck snapped with a quick twist. When are people going to learn to stop pissing me off?

It didn't take long to find Mabel's place on Benvenue Avenue. I just couldn't believe that the frumpy diner proprietor could afford to live in such a place. Then again, housing in the Bay Area was off the charts expensive. I wondered how anyone could afford to live here. I often wanted to troll neighborhoods in places like Blackhawk, knock on doors, and ask, "What the fuck exactly do you do for a living?" Investment bankers and hedge fund managers weren't *that* common. This wasn't Silicon Valley, so these neighborhoods weren't teeming with dot-com millionaires.

Berkeley was trendy, with Cal at the center of it all. If these streets and homes could talk, what stories they could tell. So much history here. I would have to get nostalgic another time.

I stood on the sidewalk staring at the triplex for a good long while as I plotted my strategy. Knocking on the door was an option, but I doubted that Mabel would open up for me. Floating outside her bedroom was a possibility, but scaring her out of her wits was for later. Lucky for me, her place had a staircase on the back side that led to the kitchen. Well, I presumed it was the kitchen. Common sense told me stairs to a door like this would lead to the kitchen. The front entrance would take me to a living or family room. Yeah, I was an architect all of a sudden.

The wooden stairs weren't old and creaky like I was used to, and that was a relief as I climbed with care and stealth. The door frame cracked as I turned the knob and threw my shoulder into it, trying to be as noiseless as possible. Tiptoeing through the apartment, I began my search for Mabel. I was right about the kitchen, and she wasn't there. It opened into the living room, and she wasn't there either. The walls and the mantle were lined with family photographs in every frame imaginable—ornate gold leaf antiques to brand-new chrome rectangles of the box-store variety.

A glass of wine, a lit candle, and a syrupy romance novel waited on the coffee table.

The telltale sound of water from a faucet caught my attention. I padded as gently as I could down the hall toward the bedrooms. Before I could reach the boudoir, I found Mabel at the sink in the bathroom. She was brushing her teeth. After rinsing and spitting one last time, Mabel looked at her reflection in the mirror. She pulled one heavy lower eyelid down and inspected a bloodshot eye.

"Hello, Mabel."

Mabel dropped the plastic tumbler she had been holding into the sink with a clatter and stared into the mirror. She knew she wouldn't see anything but her own haggard visage but she looked over her reflection's shoulder regardless.

"How did you …?"

"That's not important right now. We can do this the easy way or the hard way. It's up to you."

"I didn't mean for …"

"Uh-huh. I'm really sick and tired of people crossing me, Mabel."

"I didn't have a choice."

"I'm a little tired of that refrain, too. Shall we sit and talk or do you want to die in your bathroom?"

Mabel turned to face me. My eyes and my fangs told her trying to fight me was a bad idea. I was leaning against the doorframe with arms crossed as she slunk by me trying her damnedest not to touch me. Her shoulder brushed mine regardless, and I felt her shudder as it did. I followed her to the living room, where she plopped on the couch and tucked one leg under her. She pulled her nightgown over her knees as a trembling hand reached for the wine glass. The candlelight danced across her face as she lifted the glass to her pursed lips.

"So, Mabel, tell me, why?"

"I told you, I didn't have a choice. They were going to lock my grandson up."

"Ah, the mythical grandson. What's he into?"

Mabel stared off into space as she cradled the glass in both hands. "Dope."

"I thought Jonas helped you out with that?"

"He got himself in trouble again. Twenty years, they said. He's just a boy. A good boy ... he just can't ..." She was looking at me now, tears welling up in her doe eyes.

"Can't what? Control himself? Help himself? I can certainly commiserate. But you thought it was better to sell Jonas out? Sell me out?"

"I didn't know what else to do. They were going take the diner."

"How the fuck were they going to do that? The cops have that kind of juice?"

"I don't know." She was sobbing and her face was in her hands. "That's what they said. The diner is all I have. They said they were going to lock Connor up, and they'd see to it that I'd lose the diner. All I had to do was tell them when you guys came in the next time, and they would make it all go away."

"Well, let's see, Mabel, your diner is full of holes, you're going to need to hire some more kitchen help, and you've managed to really piss me off. So, how did this little arrangement work out for you? Tell me, who did you talk to? Was his name Tim?"

"Y-y-y-es, that was his first name, detective Ti ..."

I didn't let her finish. Before she could get his name out of her mouth, Mabel and pinot were all over the wall. Her blood sprayed across a high-school portrait of her grandson as I opened a vein in her throat. Her foot continued to twitch even after she drew her last breath. I went to the bathroom to clean up in the very sink where Mabel had brushed her teeth for the very last time. It struck me as odd that even as I used my lack of reflection to my advantage when I snuck up on her, that same condition now made it very difficult to groom myself after making a mess of Mabel.

I made do and headed out the way I'd come in. As I hit the sidewalk in front of the triplex, a wave of anger came over me. Why did these fucking people think they were better off with the authorities than me or Jonas? Why didn't Mabel talk to Jonas about her conversation with Tim? Why had she let that ass-clown manipulate her into betraying someone who had helped her? Of course, my mind wandered to Billy, who had done the same exact thing. I highly doubted that Jonas had threatened Mabel the way I had Billy. I'm sure the thought had never crossed his mind that Mabel could or would turn on him. The possibility had always been in the back of my mind with Billy; that's why I'd made it clear that I would end him, and everyone he cared about, if he crossed me. Cross me he had. And we know how that turned out.

Tim was a fucking problem. Tim had to go. I'm not stupid. For every one of him, five more ambitious cops trying to make a name for themselves would crop up in his place. But this was getting personal. He obviously knew what we were, and discretion wasn't the better part of valor when it came to his methods. I needed to pay him a visit. Him and ... what was his girl's name? Oh, yeah, Kelsi.

Wandering around Berkeley wasn't going to do me any good. Having just fed, I needed to get back to my sanctuary and formulate a plan. I also needed to find out what had happened to Jonas. Part of me felt bad that I'd left him in the diner to fend for himself. Part of me was glad I hadn't remained behind with him, because I had discovered a new ability. If he was half the vampire I thought he was, if he was half the cop I thought he was, he was just fine. But I suspected that wasn't the case, and ALL of me worried that he was dead or worse.

CHAPTER IX

I arose to the night in a panic. If I drew breath, I would have been hyperventilating. Jonas Dietrich in distress was on my brain. The events of the night before weighed on me. I needed to find Jonas. This knot in my stomach told me he was in trouble. But I didn't even know where to start to look. I pulled out my smart phone and was immediately bombarded by a flurry of news alerts.

"Disgraced SFPD detective arrested ..."

"Fugitive cop taken into custody ..."

"San Francisco PD's hotshot detective suspected of murder ..."

Oh, great, Jonas had made the national news as well. I couldn't bring myself to click on any of the links. All I could think of while I chewed on my thumb was what to do next. Blackfoot appeared out of nowhere and threw herself against my back, pushing me into a rocking motion with her nuzzling and rubbing. I tossed the phone to the side and hopped to my feet. Blackfoot didn't appreciate the extra hard pat on the head and bit my hand.

I needed a plan. I needed to find where Jonas was being held. I needed to feed. I needed a lot of things.

There was no way they'd put him in the county lockup. First of all, he was a cop—that wouldn't have gone over very well. Second, Tim had to know what he was, so I wanted to believe he wouldn't expose Jonas to sunlight. Third, unless there was a stroke of luck in my favor, a lot of cops were going to die.

I willed transformation into bat form and took flight. Before long I was flapping past Cliff House and the Sutro Baths. A twinge squeezed my belly as I hugged the rocks and cliffs along Point Lobos and Lands End. That night at the baths with Andrei and Julie was forever seared into my brain. For all intents and purposes, Julie had died that night. Even though she walked the earth once again, the Julie I knew, my childhood friend, my co-worker, my confidant, was dead. That baby-stealing *thing* was not Julie. Funny. Julie had once called me a "thing."

As I banked right and made my way to the twisting, winding Coastal Trail, I heard the faint strains of Latin music. It got louder as I got closer. It got more annoying as I got closer. It was just after sundown and for the life of me I couldn't understand why someone would be blaring music along such a hushed, pristine walking trail nestled into the very edge of California.

The Banda music was offensive to my sensitive ears in my transformed state. I had only chosen this route because I needed to think, I need to formulate my break-Jonas-out-of-jail plan. I hadn't planned on feeding just yet.

I rounded a bend and found the source of the music. Two Latinas, one older and one younger—mother and daughter maybe—were sauntering along the trail licking ice cream cones and bopping to the music that emanated from what could only be a Bluetooth speaker in the younger's backpack.

Fluttering in and out of the tree line, I turned the trunks and the limbs into a slalom course as I looked and waited for the opportune moment, the right curve, the right twisted gnarled tree trunks.

The music fueled my rage, my rage fueled my thirst.

Transforming mid-flight wasn't something I had much experience with, but I executed the maneuver just a few feet from my quarry. I made sure to shift on the seaward side of the trail so I could drive the women off the path and into a hollow between two large, twisted clumps of trees. The older woman's screams turned to gurgles in what seemed like nanoseconds as I opened her throat with the claws on my right hand while I pinned the younger to a tree trunk with my free hand.

The older woman twitched as the blood escaped her jugular vein in a torrent of thick, syrupy dark liquid. The younger strained and pushed and struggled against my hand but my arm was locked at the elbow, and the bitch wasn't

going anywhere. I squeezed her larynx, hard, making it impossible for her to utter a sound.

She continued to kick her legs and twist her body while I lapped blood from the open wound in her companion's neck. I slaked my thirst until I knew the older woman wasn't coming back from it and turned my attention to the younger. As the older woman faded into the blackness, I fished the wireless speaker out of the backpack and bashed the younger woman's face in with it until both were smashed beyond recognition.

I stood up and tossed the speaker to the side in disgust. "Fuck you both."

I didn't even try to hide the bodies or cover them up. The music alone had pissed me off and driven me to what I'd done. No respect for where they were. Nobody wanted to hear their tunes. I sure as hell didn't. I figured I'd done the world a favor, at least until the next obnoxious assholes came along to disturb the serenity.

And with that, I strolled along the path for a while until I heard hikers heading toward me from the opposite direction. I ducked into the trees and headed back toward the top of the bluff. I made my way to the Lands End lookout, sprinted into a transformation, and flew off into the night.

CHAPTER X

My money was on SFPD Central Station. It had to be where Tim was based. Hell, I couldn't even remember the fucker's last name. I flew along Vallejo Street and settled in at Ina Coolbrith Park, where I transformed. This secluded little spot was a perfect patch of nature for me to get my bearings and come up with a strategy.

I reached up and grabbed a low branch as I surveyed the area and listened. The police station was a block and a half from my locale. Assaulting the place was not an option. It might not have been Precinct 13, and they may not have known I was coming, but a violent, full-frontal attack was their method, not mine. I was a little more subtle than that, just a little.

Mason and Powell Streets were between me and the

station. I walked along Vallejo Street and crossed both streets and paused alongside a Chinese produce store. Cops came and went; police cars, black and whites and unmarked alike, were double-parked. Nobody seemed to care. Could I get lucky enough for the cops to transfer Jonas somewhere? At this very moment? Nah. But it was a nice thought.

Steeling my nerves, I put on my best smolder and pounded my way right into SFPD Central. I hoped my timing was good and since it was early evening still, maybe the station would have minimal staff on duty. I didn't want to have to mesmerize an entire shift. I found the desk sergeant in short order. He was no match for my hypnotic stare and gave up Jonas's location before his heart could beat three times. I know because I heard it. A security camera caught my attention. It swept back and forth like an oscillating fan on a hot August day. I smiled a little, knowing damn well whoever was monitoring the feed couldn't see me.

After lifting the keys from an officer and hypnotizing two others, I found Jonas in a holding cell in the back of the station. As I walked the gauntlet of cells, every movie you can think of popped into my head. From *Silence of the Lambs* to *The Dark Knight Rises*, I thought of every actor who had to take such a walk. Well, I wasn't Clarice Starling, and it wasn't Dr. Hannibal Lecter I found.

Detective Sergeant Jonas Dietrich rotated from lying on his back to sitting up and took me in. He was stunned for a long moment before he actually spoke.

"Elizabeth! What the hell are you doing here?"

"I'm Luke Sky … oh, hell, I can't pull that off. Is that any way to thank your liberator?"

Jonas stepped forward, grasped the bars with his hands, and put his face between the steel rods. I kissed him gently but quickly on the lips and proceeded to unlock the cell door.

As he shuffled out he straightened his rumpled suit and trench coat and looked down the corridor with consternation.

"Where is Tim's office?"

"Huh, w-w-why do you want to know that?"

"Jonas, where is his office?"

"This way, come on."

My hypnotized officers were still just that but we needed to move with alacrity if we were to get out before more cops returned to the station from patrol or the nearest donut shop. Jonas led me to Tim's office. After a few minutes of rummaging, I had learned a lot. I had his last name, his wife's name, her occupation and business address, and their home address.

"Come on, Elizabeth, we gotta go."

While I was rifling Tim's desk, Jonas had filched a set of car keys. He hustled me through an exit that led straight to the garage. Jonas took a minute punching remote buttons until the lights blinked and the horn chirped on a silver Crown Vic. He slipped into the driver's seat, and I dived through the passenger door. He turned the engine over, grabbed the column shifter, threw the car into reverse, screeched the tires, and the car lurched backward.

Moments later, we were on Vallejo Street headed west. We turned left on Mason and right on Broadway.

"We need to get out of the city."

"Yeah, yeah, I know. Where do you suggest? You ready to tell me where your sanctuary is?"

"Nope, not happening yet, cowboy. Let's get to Oakland. I need your sleuthing skills."

"You're the boss."

"'Bout time you admitted it. Temescal Beach House, James."

"Who's James?"

"Just fucking drive."

Jonas took a left on Taylor and doubled back. Another left on Washington finally had us headed in the right direction. Before long we were on I-80 and crossing the Bay Bridge. I was thankful for the winding route. I figured it was keeping us off the radar. Neither one of us was comfortable crossing the Bay, but it was a necessary evil. The twenty-five minute drive went by fast even though Jonas barely threatened the speed limit so we wouldn't arouse suspicion.

We took 80 to 580 and peeled north on 24 through Rockridge. That tennis court conversation we'd had seemed a million years ago. Melancholy washed over me as I gazed out the window and thought of it as we passed by the Claremont.

It was just before midnight when we reached the

Temescal Beach House. I needed any leads, any clues, as to where Sarah and Julie bedded down during the day. Detective Dietrich was good at these things. Maybe he could pick up their trail, maybe they'd left clues behind, maybe he was Fred and I was Daphne.

"We're going to have to ditch this car. It wouldn't be long before SFPD figures out where it went. These things do have GPS trackers, you know."

"Yeah, yeah. Hopefully we won't be here long. Come on, Columbo, get to sleuthin'."

"What exactly are we looking for?"

"Um … I don't know. Anything. Anything that will tell us where they stay during daylight hours. Anything that connects them to Andrei. Shit, Jonas, you're the detective. *Detect!*"

"Yeah, yeah. Got it."

Jonas pulled a flashlight out of the glove compartment of the Crown Vic and scoured the perimeter of the place while I milled about the parking lot.

"You sure made a mess of the place."

"Yeah, well. I learned full-frontal assault from your SWAT buddies."

Jonas made his way inside the event space. After a few minutes …

"Hey, Elizabeth! I think I found something."

I swooped through the doorway with much more care than the last time I had been here. The police tape wasn't much of an impediment.

"Whatcha got?"

"See this?"

He swept his flashlight's beam over the floor. Mixed in with the debris from my baby rescue operation was what looked like dirt.

"See that? That's not ordinary dirt, it's earth. There's plenty of beach sand in here too, but this dirt doesn't belong here."

"How the hell would you know that?"

"Trust me."

"Well, where did it come from? Had to be tracked in here, but by whom? Anyone could have ..."

I stopped myself in mid-thought and froze in my tracks.

"Livermore."

"What? What's in Livermore?"

"Well, my dear detective, I was born and raised there. So was Julie. Where was her funeral? Where was she buried?"

"I didn't exactly go to the service, Elizabeth, I was too busy trying to cover for you."

"Details, details. I'd bet money she was buried at Roselawn."

"We're going to have to swap vehicles. I'm not hitting the freeway in that thing again."

"I'm pretty sure you can't fly, so .... and I am never hitchhiking again."

"Why not?"

"Long story."

This was one of those times when I wished Dietrich had embraced his nature and developed some abilities. I really wanted to shift into bat form and flap my way to Livermore but never got the impression that Jonas knew how to do such things, nor was he interested in learning. I had a sinking feeling that these abilities manifested solely as fight or flight responses for all vampires, not just me. For some reason, Jonas had never been compelled to shift or transform or whatever you wanted to call it.

Regardless, we needed to get to Livermore. If my hunch was correct, we'd find Julie's resting place at Roselawn, and maybe even Sarah's if they were truly in cahoots. And I had a mind to find out what my brothers were up to, and the only way to ascertain that was to pay a visit to my parents' house.

I wasn't sure what I was going to find there. The last time I was in the neighborhood I thought my brothers saw me lurking. I wished in my heart of hearts that I could approach them, talk to them, explain. But I was better off dead. They didn't need to know what I had become. They didn't need to know what I had done. They really didn't need to know that I had killed our parents. I rubbed my belly absentmindedly. This was a habit now every time I thought of the one shot my father had gotten off. The hole he'd blown in his daughter's stomach before she brutally murdered him.

Yeah, my brothers were better off not knowing any of this.

CHAPTER XI

"So, you don't know how to shift?"

"Huh, what? What do you mean 'shift?'"

"You know, transform, turn into something. You know, like Andrei and the fog? Me and bats and other ... um ... critters?"

"Oh .... um ... well, I never really thought about it. You and Andrei and your abilities, I don't know if I can ... you know ... what did you call it? Shift?"

"Yeah. I have transformed into a bat, a wolf, a horde of rats, and smoke or mist or whatever. I pretty much can transform into a bat whenever I like. I can also, I don't know, commune with certain creatures."

"Commune?"

"Yeah. I can sort of 'mind-meld' with spiders and bats

and such, see as they see. Comes in handy for recon and surveillance."

"I'd say. And how exactly did you discover these 'abilities?'"

"That's an interesting question. I'll explain on the way to Livermore after we jack this car."

"Huh? What?"

I noticed a vehicle approaching in my periphery. Its headlights were blinding.

"Shhhh, duck."

Dietrich and I hid behind the Crown Vic as a compact coupe pulled into the parking lot. The car found a spot in the darkest part of the lot before the driver threw it into park. The red brake lights flickered briefly.

"Stay here, Jonas. I got this."

"What … wait … Elizabeth! What are you doing?"

"Trust me," I said with a wink and a coy grin.

Smoothing myself as I went, I strutted over to what turned out to be a yet another Hyundai Accent. Before the driver could open the door, I put on my best congenial smile and tapped on the window. The driver reluctantly pushed the power window button and only allowed the window down far enough to have a conversation.

"Help you?"

"Yeah, um, hi. How's it going?"

"Fine, just fine. What the hell do you want?"

He was in his mid-twenties and so was his little chippie blonde girlfriend. He wasn't unattractive, a little scruffy with dark hair and stubble. His girl was underdressed for the season. Short skirt, tight off-the-shoulder top. It had long sleeves but she didn't have a jacket or a coat. A quick visual scan of the backseat indicated no coat. I thought maybe she was a hooker. Either way, this couple had come here for one reason and one reason alone. I couldn't care less; I needed their car.

"Yeah, see my friend over there? Well, we need your car. And you're going to give it to us."

"Excuse me?"

"You heard me."

"Listen, bitch," the hussy in the passenger seat spewed as she leaned over the driver. "I don't know who you think you are, but me and Thatcher don't have to take your bullshit."

"Shut up, McKenzie."

"Oh, Thatcher, eh? And what was it, McKenzie?" A deliciously warm, malicious laugh emanated from my throat. "You can have that Crown Vic over there to do whatever it is you're going to do. Or you can cut through the crime scene over there and go fuck on the beach, I don't give a rat's ass. But we're taking your Accent."

"The fuck you are."

Thatcher reached for the ignition switch. I grabbed the door handle and yanked the driver's door open. The hinge caught and swung the door into my thigh and hip. With my left hand, I pushed the door away and held it while I grabbed Thatcher with my right hand and tried to pull him out of the vehicle. His seatbelt was still fastened. "God-dammit." I let go of his shirt collar and reached down to release the seat belt latch. As I pushed the button I happened to glance in Dietrich's direction. Jonas put his hands out, palms up, and shrugged his shoulders.

"What?"

"Nothing. You said you got this. I'm just waiting for you to do whatever it is you're going to do. I'm in no rush."

"Well, you could help me."

"Oh, now you want my help. A minute ago you had it all under control."

"This squirmy fucker isn't cooperating."

And Thatcher was squirming. He was flopping around like a fish that didn't want to be tossed into the bucket. He was thrashing and kicking as I dragged him by the collar away from his car and his girl. McKenzie got out of the car and hustled around the back end of it.

"Elizabeth! Look out!"

Jonas's warning came too late, and McKenzie cold-cocked me in the back of the head with a piece of drift-wood. I really didn't want to hurt these kids, I just wanted their car. Again, Jonas threw up his hands and shrugged.

"You bitch, you leave him alone!"

The bit of wood upside the head pissed me off more than anything else. It was going to take more than that to hurt me, but it sure got my attention.

"Spunky little thing you are. I mean you no harm. Just give up the car, and we'll go in peace."

"Fuck you. You can't have it. Now, let him go!"

I bared my fangs and hissed, while one impossibly long and sharp nail extended from my index finger and threatened Thatcher's throat.

In a deep, resonant voice I barely recognized as my own, I said, *"Drop the wood and back off, or I will slit his throat."* My claw nail played across the gooseflesh on Thatcher's throat; McKenzie's next words caught in her throat as she struggled to grasp the situation.

"Not so tough, are you, honey? Put it down and I'll let him go."

"O-o-kay. Whatever you say, just let us go. Leave us alone."

McKenzie crouched down slowly, deliberately, and placed what looked like an eroded tree branch on the ground. Tears were streaming down her face, creating mascara rivers over her cheekbones. She held out her hands in a supplicating gesture.

"Please, let us go. Please."

Her sobbing was only interrupted by gasps for air. Thatcher had stopped squirming and was now just lying limp at my boot heels, half sitting up only because I held him that way by his collar.

I looked over at Jonas. Once again, he shrugged. He looked bored.

"Are you not amused?"

"You should have just killed them."

"W-w-w-what?" McKenzie stammered.

"Oh, he's just kidding, honey, sort of. Aren't'cha, Jonas?"

The fact of the matter was I could have killed these two whenever I felt like it, although I had no real reason to. They were just a couple of kids looking for a backseat romp. It wasn't their fault they'd come upon a pair of vampires with a need and an agenda.

"C'mon, Jonas, let's go."

Dietrich thrust his hands in his pockets, strolled around the police cruiser, and casually walked toward the Accent. He blew an air kiss in my direction as he passed me.

"Ass."

Jonas waited in the passenger seat while I mesmerized the lovebirds.

"... you will remember none of what has transpired this evening. Go to the beach and fuck like rabbits."

Stunned but compliant, Thatcher and McKenzie made their way past the police tape and into the event space, then headed for the man-made lake. I slipped into the driver's seat and turned the engine over. I looked to my right to find Jonas staring at me.

"What?"

"You're something else, you know that?"

"You may not like what you are, Jonas, but I am done apologizing for what I am. I can do things, affect things, and I refuse to be ashamed of it or hide it."

"Okay, then, drive."

And with that, I willed the Accent into motion, and its tires spit and spewed gravel as we pulled out of the parking lot out onto the paved road and sped off into the night.

"How did you develop all of these ... skills?"

"Practice, Jonas, practice. I have spent many a night, countless hours figuring out how to commune with the children of the night. We are of them. Why fight it? As for the shifting, well, like I said, that was fight or flight. But each time I shifted into a new form, I found I could do it again if need be if I concentrated hard enough. How do you think I found you and Da Rocha that night?"

"I never really thought about it. He and I were in the middle of one helluva fight when you showed up."

"Well, the damn headaches and nosebleeds took some doing to get under control. But they're minimal now. I used every creature I could to find Da Rocha. It just so happened he was going toe-to-toe with you."

"I still don't think we should have killed him. He's not the only one, you know. His death is going to come back on us."

"He had to go, Jonas. I was sick and tired of him getting the drop on me. It was either him or me. If there are more like him, let them come."

"It's not that simple."

"Nothing ever is. Andrei needs to go too. I thought I'd finished him once, and we gave him a pass for helping with Da Rocha. But I'll never be free until I destroy him."

"You don't think I want Andrei dead too? I have more reason than you do."

"I never said you didn't. Look, the bottom line is this. Neither one of us will be able to exist in peace, we'll never be able to forge our fucked-up lives through this reality, until that asshole is gone. Agreed?"

After a long pause and contemplative staring out the passenger window ...

"... Agreed."

"Good. Now, let's get to Livermore and see if we can't figure some shit out. First, let's find Julie's sanctuary."

I guided the car to I-580 and navigated past I-238 through San Leandro into Dublin and Pleasanton. It was a good thing that I'd decided to drive. I could feel my OCD starting to rise, and it was easier to resist the urge to count everything while I concentrated on the road. Before long, we started to see the first few Livermore exits. I took the N. Livermore exit and turned right.

After crossing Las Positas, I made the left into Roselawn. A large dark slab with the words "Roselawn Cemetery" chiseled into the marble that sat atop a stone retaining wall marked the entrance. A wrought iron fence formed a perimeter around the property.

None of what I saw looked familiar even though Roselawn had served as my sanctuary for some time. My memories of that time were clouded. I had been more worried about Andrei and what he had turned me into than I was geography and topography. Waking up with a dead child in my arms and massacring boutique shoppers were bigger concerns than cemetery master planning. The only crypt construction that mattered to me was the one I found in which to hole up.

Now I had to pay attention, now I had to look for clues and signs. I was pretty sure that I had covered my tracks but Andrei had been able to find me. Maybe he was able to sense his progeny, or, more likely, he followed me. From ornate obelisks shaped like the Washington Monument to intricate carved wooden totems, markers of any and all varieties dotted the burial grounds. Judging from the girls' incompetence demonstrated so far, I didn't think it would be too difficult to find their crypt. "Their," because I assumed Julie and Sarah would be bunking down together.

If they were anything like I had been at this point, they would be scared and desperate. Unless Andrei was helping them make their way. It was really starting to look like that was unlikely, but I couldn't rule it out. Roselawn had worked for me as an early hiding place. I probably would have stayed longer had I not needed to find Dietrich and if Andrei had not found me.

I wasn't exactly sure what I was going to do if we did find their hiding place. There was little chance that they would be there given the time of night. I thought maybe we could befoul the crypt or the sarcophagi to draw them out, but then again, how the hell were we going to handle the religious objects with which to do that? I wasn't touching a Eucharist wafer or a crucifix, no fucking way. Finding the resting place was the priority; the plan would have to come later.

"We'll cover more ground if we split up, Jonas."

"What exactly are we looking for?"

"You're the detective, you tell me."

"Well, the signs should be obvious. Crypts disturbed, especially the entry doors and slabs."

"I doubt they are very sophisticated. I don't get the impression that subtlety is one of their strong suits."

We split up and headed in opposite directions. Every few rows of graves, I glanced to see where he was, and each time I caught him looking at me. I made a wordless gesture of insistence that told him to concentrate on the task at hand and not on what I was doing. I passed several rows of military headstones. The graves were marked with tiny American flags. I caught myself humming *God Bless America* as I stepped lightly and quickly past these interred heroes.

Thirty-eight, in case you were wondering. Dammit.

The cemetery was pitch-black with even blacker shadows. A quick breeze rustled leaves, swirling them around the roots of a solitary tree. Those leaves, dry and brittle, flew across the threshold of a crypt. After spinning up into a tornado of dead foliage, they were sucked into that stone structure. The mausoleum was built into the side of a hill. I take that back; it looked like it *grew* out of the hill.

Dried leaves of orange and brown crunched under my boots as I made my way to the stone steps of the crypt. I crept and stepped lightly as I approached the wrought iron gate, which was, of course, ajar. Jonas was off God knows where. I should have called for him or signaled him somehow. I didn't know if I was going to need backup. There was no way Julie or Sarah was here. I couldn't get that lucky, especially with the first structure I chose to inspect.

Nonetheless, I slipped in between the large heavy wooden doors, left parted just far enough for me to slither inside without having to push them further apart, which would have made such a racket. The bottom of the one door that had been moved had left quite the drag mark. Something told me it wouldn't be easy to move. These old crypts were in disrepair and their door hinges were worn and rusty. It always blew my mind in movies like *Indiana Jones* or *The Mummy* when the ancient mechanism worked flawlessly like the day it was constructed. This mausoleum was only a few hundred years old, and I knew deep down I would've needed to use some serious force to get into it had I found it undisturbed.

Step by agonizing step, I walked toward the sarcophagi. The walls were lined with stone vaults, bunk-bed style, Navy ship coffin-rack style. Two more large stone vaults sat in the middle of the space. The lids were off, slid to the side, and the voids revealed relatively new metal coffins. They looked like 1940's automobiles with matte finishes and chrome accents. Those lids were open as well and the satin pillows and sheets were luxurious and inviting. I ran my fingers along the stone and then dragged them across the soft, smooth material. I thought of the abandoned church I had called home; I thought of my own "death," of the internment that never happened.

I felt something on my shoulder. I spun around.

"Fuck, Jonas. Really?"

"Sorry, you seemed lost in sneaking."

"I was, but Jesus, don't *you* sneak up on me like that."

"Geez, you're wound tight."

"Yeah, well, I'm not sure what we're going to find in here, if anything, and I don't want any more surprises."

I made a face at him, like "uh," so he knew that was the last of the surprises for the night.

Once we quieted our minds and our mouths, we heard it. A soft suckling sound. A sound we knew all too well. In the recess in the back of the crypt, in the space that was carved out of the hill ... a figure ... a feminine form ... crouched down ... hunched over ...

"Hey!" Jonas barked.

"Sarah."

The real-estate-agent-turned-bloodsucker craned her neck and tilted her head in our direction. Crimson liquid poured out of her mouth and dripped from her fangs. My gaze moved from her face to her victim. A mewling child, a girl, of no more than three or four years old, dressed in nothing but a nightgown. No coat, no shoes or socks. Two streams of blood flowed from the wounds in her throat.

The fiend stood up and held the child by the wrist. She stared at us dumbfounded. The thirst had her. Her mouth was agape as she languished in her stupor. The girl dangled and began to shriek as she emerged from her trance-like state. The strain on the poor kid's shoulder had to be excruciating. I thought her arm was going to pop out of the socket.

"SARAH!"

My voice must have resonated with her, because her head snapped to and her eyes locked on to mine. It took her a moment to snap out of her stupefied bloodlust. When she did, and when she realized that it was me, she dropped the child like a sack of potatoes. The girl landed with a sharp smack on the stone slab of a floor and immediately began to wail. Tears streamed down her cherub-like face, and she kicked her feet. Her hair was tousled and matted, and her nightgown was torn in several places.

"Jonas," I breathed.

"On it."

While Sarah was fixated on me, Dietrich moved with alacrity and scooped the little girl up into his arms. He wrapped his coat around her and held her tightly to his chest. "Shhhhhh."

"Go, get her out of here."

"But where?"

"I don't know." I tossed my head toward the doors. "Do I look like I give a damn? Get the fuck out of here."

Jonas hustled past me, through the doors and out into the night. My attention never strayed from Sarah. I looked her up and down, from head to toe. She was impeccably dressed, but it was an illusion. Upon closer inspection, from the neck up, she was a fucking mess. Her hair flew from the sides of her head like Bozo the Clown's. Blood stained her chin, her chest, and her blouse. One of her heels had broken off. The strap on the other shoe had given way as well.

"Seriously, Sarah, what the fuck have you done?"

"What do you know, Elizabeth? Huh? This is all your fault."

"My fault? Boy, do you have your wires crossed. That baby, the one in Berkeley … that had nothing to do with Andrei, did it? That was for you two idiots."

"Yeah, well, what's your point? We're not as advanced as you, we're not as *evolved* as you. It is your fault. You made me, that night at my house, in the shower … I fell in love with you. I tasted you. And now you've spoiled my dinner."

Her words stung. They didn't make any sense either. I knew she had been tainted by Andrei, but obviously, that night I'd spent in her house … something had happened in her shower, something I didn't quite recall. Something I didn't exactly dislike. But I still couldn't remember how or why she'd tasted my blood or whatever it was that *made* her.

And what did she mean that she wasn't as advanced or as evolved? There hadn't been that much time between when I was made and when she and Julie were turned. Maybe I'd worked at developing my abilities more than they did. But Sarah could transform; I'd seen her do it. Why she felt the need to prey on young children, babies even, well, that was the sixty-four thousand dollar question, wasn't it?

"Where's Julie?"

"None of your fuckin' business."

"Oh? Seems like you two are a couple of peas in a pod, right down to the matching coffins."

"We're doing what we have to do. What we have to do to survive. Not that you've been any help in that regard."

"Am I supposed to hold your hand, tell you what to do? Hate to tell you this, but I'm making this shit up as I go along. It's not like becoming a vampire came with a fucking instruction manual. And Andrei wasn't exactly a mentor. What I can tell you is this. Stop eating KIDS!"

"Why? They're easy, and oh, so sweet. It's not like you'd know … wait a minute …"

I broke eye contact with Sarah and cast my gaze at the floor. My experience with children was speaking loudly and clearly without my having to say a word, and she knew it. It was written all over my face.

"Aha! I knew it!"

First my head and then my eyes lifted to meet hers again.

"That's why I'm telling you—it's wrong on so many levels, You won't be able to live … with yourself. Trust me."

"I'm doing just fine, BETH!"

She spat my name at me. Well, that which I hated anyway.

"Bitch, nobody, and I mean nobody calls ME BETH!"

With that, Sarah turned toward the back of the crypt, to the void, to the empty space where Jonas and I had found her feeding on the child, hunched down, and burst through an opening that wasn't readily apparent. These old mausoleums were full of surprises. By the time I scrambled over the top of one of the stone coffin vaults and gave chase, Sarah was gone. For several moments I stood on top of the hill that had sprouted the crypt and surveyed the cemetery in every direction. There was no sign of my deranged progeny.

Before long Dietrich sidled up next to me.

"What do you want me to do with her?"

"I don't know, Jonas, take her to the nearest police station, I guess. Drop her on the doorstep. I'm sure there has to be a missing person's report out on her."

I put my index finger to his lips before he could say another word. "Shhhhh. Stop talking. Meet me at my parents' house."

I opened Dietrich's coat and stroked the little girl's cheek.

"You okay, honey?"

She nodded nervously and nuzzled up tightly against Jonas's chest.

"Go, Jonas."

And with that, my dear detective headed off to a safe place to deposit the little girl.

CHAPTER XII

The walk to my parents' house was uneventful. When I say that I mean nothing happened. That doesn't mean that my mind wasn't racing with a million thoughts. I couldn't help but think about the last few times I had been here and the events that had transpired. Once again I absentmindedly rubbed my belly. Sure, the wound had healed thanks to my preternatural abilities, but what about the gaping rip in my soul, if I had one, considering I had murdered my parents and my father had shot his only daughter in the middle of the slaughter?

The car I took and where and how I ended up leaving it weighed on me as well. The events in the days and weeks after my *becoming* played on the movie screen in my mind as I trudged to my folks' house. My brothers being back in town weighed on me. As usual, I had more questions than answers.

Why were they here? What did they want? Was there an issue with their inheritance? Was my missing corpse causing them any issues? Had they spoken to Jonas's cop buddy Tim?

All of these questions and more flipped and rolled through my mind as I approached the house.

I was alarmed by what I saw.

Three large black SUVs were parked in the street in front of the house. Two huskies with automatic assault rifles slung were stationed at the front door, while another paced in front of the garage door. They looked like military or mercenaries. They were too well put together and sharp to be Livermore PD. I highly doubted that they were SFPD. This was way out of their jurisdiction.

The license plates on the SUVs were European style, long in the horizontal, but all they said in addition to the alpha-numeric was "EXEMPT." No country or state of origin, just "EXEMPT." Now, I had traveled a little bit, and I have seen European license plates, and I have seen tags from numerous states, but never had I seen a blanket "EXEMPT" with no state, county, or country of origin. Even diplomatic tags would have a country flag on them, something.

I stood under a tree a few houses down, surveying the situation. I felt a hand on my shoulder …

"Goddammit, Jonas, what did I tell you about sneaking up on me?!?"

"Sorry."

"What did you do with the kid?"

"Exactly what you said to do. What's the haps?"

"What's the haps? You did not just say that to me."

"Isn't that how the kids ... ?"

"Oh, Jonas, your fuddy-duddyness is one of your most endearing qualities. You are a throwback to a different time; stay that way."

I gently double-slapped him on the cheek. "Here's looking ... "

"You really don't have to finish that sentence."

If we hadn't been surveilling these black ops types, we would have busted out laughing.

"Did you see the Crown Vic up the street?"

"No, I was more concerned with the black SUVs and the mercs at the door."

"Ah, yes. Well, it looks like SFPD to me."

"I knew I smelled a rat."

"If I were a betting man, I'd say Tim is in there with these paramilitary thugs."

"Great, just what I need. There's only one way to find out."

"And just how, pray tell, are we going to do that?"

Without saying another word, I reached into a jacket pocket and pulled out an impossibly small bat. Kitti's hog-nosed bat.

The smallest mammal in the world. It twitched and trembled in my hand. Bumblebee bats weren't indigenous to California. Hell, these damn things weren't even from this continent, but somehow, this little lady had found her way to me. Yes, she was female. I was used to bats finding their way from Mexico and Southern California, and I knew that bats were drawn to me, but this was a tad ridiculous. Zoo escapee, maybe. However, I'd known she was going to serve a purpose, so before we'd headed out and met up for the night, I had tucked her in a pocket.

I stroked her back gently as she crawled and twitched along my index finger. Something shifted as I made a mental connection with this infinitesimal flying goddess. She buzzed off into the milky blackness of the night and made for the chimney of my parents' house, the chimney that held so many Christmas dreams of Santa, the chimney that funneled the smoke from countless evening fires into Livermore's purple sky (even on Spare the Air days), the chimney that carried the smoke from hundreds of melted and burnt s'mores marshmallows.

The tiny little bat fluttered her way down into the hearth guided by my mental urgings. She listened for the loudest sounds and flew in that direction. A few twists and turns later, she landed in the corner of the dining room ceiling in the crown molding joint. I willed her to make herself as small as possible.

" … are you out of your fucking mind, detective? How in the hell is my, our, sister still alive?!?!"

It seemed like we'd entered this meeting pretty close to

the beginning. Paolo was the more hotheaded of my brothers. He was pacing and ranting at Jonas's old pal Tim, who stood in a corner with his arms crossed. Tim's jaw was set, and he was looking through the dining room table to the floor. Stavros sat at the table, staring at the wood grain and tracing the lines in the maple with his index finger. His dram of Scotch was nearly empty.

Paolo continued his pacing and his ranting while three large paramilitary types sat at the table. They were dressed in black, their weapons were slung across their backs, and all three held coffee mugs between their meaty hands. An older man sat at the head of the table. He was dressed in a black three-piece suit, a light gray dress shirt, and a blood red necktie, which was tied with a tulip knot. His elbows were on the table, and his fingers were interlaced; he rested his chin on his knuckles as he listened.

"What the fuck do you mean by 'undead?', detective? What does that even mean?"

"We believe ... myself, and a few other cops in the department, and of course, the members of the Order present tonight ... that your sister is a vampire."

"Get the fuck out of here! There's no such thing. Vampires don't exist. That's a myth, a folktale, a fairy tale. My sister was murdered, that's all there is to it."

My sisters-in-law shuttled between the kitchen and the dining room, bringing more food and drink and clearing plates as if this were some sort of warped Thanksgiving dinner.

Ariana, Stavros's wife, refilled the dram. He grabbed her arm as she tried to walk away. "Leave the bottle." Ariana placed the bottle next to his glass and leaned down to kiss him. Stavros didn't move, so Ariana pecked him on the side of his forehead and went back to the kitchen with Paolo's wife, Sasha.

The mercs and the suit were stoic as they listened to Tim detail what he thought he knew about Andrei, Dietrich, and yours truly. He wasn't too far off. He was missing many key details, but he had the gist, and I got the impression he'd had Jonas figured a long time ago. But Paolo, God love him, he just couldn't get it through his thick skull that this was even conceivable, let alone possible.

"I'm sorry, I can't wrap my head around all of this, detective. Who the fuck is Andrei? And if you knew this Dietrich character was dirty, why didn't you do something about it?"

Poor Paolo. He just couldn't, wouldn't accept the possibilities, no, the probabilities here. While Stavros was contemplative and appeared to be taking it all in, Paolo ranted and raved and gesticulated like a wild man.

Tim told what he knew from the beginning and explained my kidnapping, Dietrich's obsession with Andrei, Julie's death, and the crimes Andrei and I were suspected of committing. Paolo grabbed fistfuls of his hair and pulled his fingers through hard and fast.

"Not my sister, man, not Elizabeth. She's not a murderer. There's no way she could have done this shit.

She's our sister." Paulo ended that last statement with a pleading look at his brother, my brother, Stavros. He rubbed his dram between his hands.

"There's no such things as vampires," Stavros said flatly, just above a whisper.

"Yeah, well, Stavr … may I call you Stavros?"

"No, you may not."

"Um … er … okay, Mr. Rubis, that's what I thought. I didn't believe it myself, but the more I investigated these killings, the more I got to know about my own colleague, the more it became the only explanation."

"Elizabeth is dead! Our parents are dead!" Paolo shouted as tears streamed down his olive complexion.

Ever the calm one, Stavros said, "There's no way our sister could have, or would have, killed our parents. She loved them, especially Pop."

A headache started to creep in, and my head developed a twitch. "You okay?" Dietrich asked, but I held up a hand that clearly meant "leave me alone." I could not afford to break the psychic connection with my little bat buddy/spy gadget. I didn't know how long I could hold it, but I knew I had to hang on. We needed all the information we could get, and I still didn't know who the jokers in black were.

"We have found, um, resting places in several locations and with the help of Mr. Tobias and his, ahem, team, we were able to sanitize them."

Now we were getting somewhere. But the thought of my resting places befouled by these assholes pissed me off.

"What the fuck do you mean 'sanitize?' Our sister isn't some vermin, she's not a virus or, or, or, a bacteria you can just Lysol away. Fuck! Stav, how much longer are we going to have to listen to this shit?" Paolo pounded on the heavy wood table and looked at our sibling in a way I had never seen.

"Try to relax, brother, we need to hear them out. We promised we would."

"But this is ludicrous ..."

Stavros held his hand up to Paolo exactly the way I just done to Jonas. Nah, we weren't related. Stavros took a long pull on his Scotch. "Continue."

"Vampires need to rest by day. It appears your sister has created strategically located ... nests. Places she can get to in a pinch if she's in trouble or if she's up against the sunrise."

"What about this Andrei character?" Stavros had taken control of the conversation, while Paolo stood in the corner running his fingers through his thick, wavy jet-black hair.

"We haven't found any such resting places that indicate they belong to him. Dietrich believed he was very old, well over a hundred years old. Your sister is more of a spree killer, while Andrei is more calculated, cunning."

"And who or what is a Serge?"

"Mr. Tobias?" Tim nodded his head toward the man at the head of the table. He was perhaps seventy years old; his skin was deeply lined, tan. Slicked back, expertly trimmed silver hair. On his right ring finger he wore a signet ring, black onyx as far as I could tell, with a silver lightning bolt inlaid. On his left wrist an Omega Seamaster, silver with a black face. His suit, Dolce and Gabbana, if I had to guess, fit him like a glove. He looked like a cultured Marlboro Man, sans cowboy hat, not to put too fine a point on him.

His voice was deep and resonant, and he was measured and chose his words carefully when he finally spoke. It was smooth like fine buttery leather, yet firm and insistent. Tobias didn't look at you so much as look through you as if his sight could penetrate the veil.

"The Jews believe that Eve was not Adam's first mate," he began, dulcet tones smooth like an eighteen-year-old Scotch. "The stories and ancient texts are a bit confla ..."

"But we're not Jewi ..." Paolo blurted.

Tobias raised two fingers and closed his eyes. Paolo knew not to interrupt again.

"There was another, Lilith. The font from which all vampires sprang. The source. A demon straight from the depths of Hell. Every culture on earth has been infested by her spawn at one time or another throughout human history. Serge Da Rocha was the finest hunter we've ever trained. He faced down countless species of this scourge. And your sister killed him. Drank from him. Fed on him."

Rage welled up inside Paolo. He was pacing again. Veins pulsed and protruded from his forehead and temples. He pounded on the table with both fists and got in Tobias's face.

"Get the fuck outta here, man! What the hell are you talking about? Our sister is dead, her body was stolen, our parents are dead. That's all there is to it. I'm not buying this religious mumbo-jumbo."

"You're repeating yourself. And just who do you think stole her body, Mr. Rubis? Hmmmm?"

Paolo grabbed fistfuls of his hair again and yanked. He was pacing once more.

"I dunno, man, some creeper who, who, you know! Whaddayacallit?"

"Necrophiliac," Paolo's wife Sasha deadpanned from the kitchen.

"Yeah, yeah, that's it. Stav, can you believe this? Are you listening to this bullshit?"

Stavros stared into the distance as if he too could pierce the veil and see into the void. But he had just let his vision blur while he stewed and simmered, trying to process this information.

"Quiet P. Let him tell it."

Tobias laid it all out, and I mean all of it. How he knew what he knew was beyond me. He knew about Andrei and the stalking since childhood, he knew about my kidnapping and the becoming, he knew about Julie and Sarah and all of my kills. I almost lost the connection with the bumblebee bat, I was so taken aback by the man's comprehensive knowledge of my entire situation. His retelling of Whitney's tale almost brought me to tears. He told of Jonas and his tragic tale.

Undoubtedly, Tim had provided what information he had. I made mental a note to deal with him later.

Tobias continued.

"We are the Order of Ohrmazd, or Ahura Mazda, if you prefer. We hunt the minions and creations of Ahriman."

"Sounds like a bad Japanese car, if you ask me," Paolo mumbled, almost under his breath.

"Scoff if you like. This is a fight as old as time. As old as humanity. It is the only fight. Light versus darkness. Good versus evil. Everything else is provincial, inconsequential. Empires crumble, nations fall. Good. Evil. These are not bedtime stories told to frighten children. These entities are not myths or legends. These are not beliefs, gentlemen … and ladies … these truths simply are."

Ariana had been leaning against the wall between the kitchen and the dining room. She listened intently while debating whether or not to interrupt and refill her husband's glass. The bottle she had left on the table was now empty, and she was clutching a fresh one. Ariana was a vision. Long, curly brown hair with golden highlights, hourglass figure, and legs that … well, you get the idea.

"Look, I may have skipped a few too many Sunday School classes to go smoke behind the church, but I know enough to know that Hell and the devil don't exist, or least they have been rendered powerless. Jesus's resurrection saw to that."

Stavros looked at his wife in astonishment while she poured more Scotch. She smiled and winked at him.

Tobias smiled, just a little, and huffed, just a little.

"Mrs. Rubis. The churches of the world have spent

decades, nay, centuries, legislating the devil and Hell out of their collective dogma. Makes the path to Heaven easier, I suppose. I do not have the time to explain all that I know or all that I and my team have seen. But know this. Your sister, if we do not destroy her, will kill you and everyone you love. Her first instinct was to come home. And you see how that turned out. She has yet to tame her thirst. Until she does, we have the advantage. The good detective here has put in a call to some allies at the state capital. We'll have carte blanche to do what we need to."

The occupants of the room looked at each other and exchanged furtive glances. A dark, uneasy understanding fell over the group.

"More coffee, Mr. Tobias?" Sasha asked.

"Please. And one more thing. Where are your children?"

Stavros took the lead on this one. "Not here. They're with their grandparents. Sasha and Ariana's folks."

Paolo had taken up a seat away from the table in an extra dining chair in the opposite corner from the entrance to the kitchen. He was slumped over. Emotions appeared to have washed over him and drained his energy. He seemed to be lost in thought.

Paolo was choking back sobs when he asked, "What do we do now?"

"You … do nothing. My team will set up surveillance and security on the house. You will all have to stay here until this matter is resolved or the threat has left the geographic area. We will liaise with the good detective here and coordinate our efforts with the San Francisco Police Department and the appropriate state agencies, along with religious leaders."

"Sounds Herculean, and we sound like bait," Stavros stated.

Rising to his feet and ignoring my brother's comment, Tobias made a circular whirlybird gesture with one hand and with the other, slugged down his hot cup of fresh coffee in one long swallow.

The three members of his team who had been sitting at the table hopped up and galvanized into action. The two guards on the front door nodded as their comrades went to their vehicles and started unloading gear. The third outdoor merc walked the perimeter. With an eerie efficiency, and an additional three female team members who had been waiting in the SUVs, they had their surveillance equipment installed and up and running in no time. They looked like paramilitary ghost hunters from some late night cable TV show. Before you knew it, motion detectors and cameras were mounted and doing their electronic jobs, monitors were switched on, and headphones were placed on heads over ears.

"But they don't show up on camera, do they?" Ariana asked.

"No, but the creatures they command do."

Stavros's wife could only manage a weak, "Oh," in response. She looked at her husband, raised her eyebrows, and rolled her eyes as she paced. The four people, well, five, who shared the name Rubis watched as the Order of Ahura Mazda went about their work. Within half an hour, the place was locked up tight against intruders—vampiric and human. They all but installed a doorbell camera.

Fuckers.

CHAPTER XIII

On one hand, I was angry that my parents' house had been turned into a three-ring CIA circus. I half expected James Bond to show up. On the other, I felt like I had the upper hand for the first time in a long time. I knew what they were up to, I knew what I was up against, and I knew the full extent of it. I willed the bumblebee bat up and out through the chimney and released the tenuous mental connection. She was disoriented and flew haphazardly until she regained her faculties and disappeared into the night.

"Come on, Jonas, we need to go."

"Yeah, yeah we do."

A few joggers and dog walkers were making their way through the neighborhood. We were conspicuous enough as it was. Jonas instinctively thrust his elbow out and I reluctantly took it, wrapping my arm around his. Better to blend in than stand out with the mercs milling around across the street.

We strolled back to the cemetery. I even lay my head to rest on Jonas's shoulder at one point. I wasn't sure if it was part of the ruse or a romantic gesture. Maybe it was comforting. I decided it was all three as we found our way back to the boosted Accent. I wondered if the original occupants were indeed fucking like rabbits, or if they had jammed off, scared out of their wits. A fleeting thought blitzed through my mind ... that maybe, just maybe, I'd like to with my escort.

The windshield wiper in my mind squeegeed that idea away as quickly as it formed. After everything we had been through, what we had done, and what we are, I was stunned that the thought of traditional intercourse was intriguing. It was a good thing that I hadn't lost interest completely.

"What are we going to do now, Jonas?"

"That's a tough question. We need to go somewhere and talk this out. How 'bout your spot?"

"Nice try, cowboy. I'm not ready for that. Your pal burned us, so the diner isn't an option. Something tells me you have somewhere we can put in. Not all of your 'safe houses' have been compromised."

There was a long pause until Jonas finally answered in a slow drawl.

"Yeah. I suppose I have a place we can go."

"Good."

CHAPTER XIV

I t was well after midnight by the time we got into San Francisco. Dietrich barely noticed my mini panic attack as we crossed the spans of the Bay Bridge. I made him drive since this was his safe house. It was a pleasant night, still, and the sky was full of stars. @Karl-TheFog must have taken the night off.

We didn't talk much, and I spent most of the time staring out the window, trying to both recover from my extended commune with the bumblebee bat and process what I'd learned. Jonas had been the lookout, and he didn't hear and see what I did.

Dietrich navigated the streets deftly and casually worked his way around the seemingly constant construction. He guided the car to Nob Hill, Jones Street, to be exact.

He parked the car; we exited the vehicle and stood on the sidewalk for a moment. He looked a nondescript, beige, seven-story building up and down. It had fire escapes facing the street on every level. It reminded me of Steve's apartment building. It reminded me of my recent fire escape-climbing exploits.

"You know Kerouac wrote *On the Road* near here."

"I did not know that."

"Yup, used to diddle Neal Cassady's wife, with Neal's permission, of course."

"Of course." I rolled my eyes. I didn't need a Beat Generation history lesson just then.

Another long pause.

"Why don't you just float up?"

"Very funny, Elizabeth, very funny. Come on, follow me and keep quiet."

Dietrich punched in a code into a keypad mounted to the wall next to the main entry door. A buzzer sounded followed by a loud click. He pulled the door open and ushered me inside.

"Fourth floor, take the stairs."

I found the doorway to the stairwell and pulled. He reached up above me and grabbed the edge of the door, holding it for both of us. I scrambled up the stairs with Dietrich close behind until we reached a landing with a large "4" painted in big red block on the wall next to another door. We eased our way through that opening and found ourselves in a well-appointed hallway. Tasteful wallpaper, large potted plants, chrome domes mounted to the ceiling that undoubtedly concealed security cameras. I flipped one of them off.

"Real mature, Liz."

I shrugged him off as he fished for a set of keys.

"Here we are, this is me."

Apartment 409.

He inserted a key into the lock and turned. The deadbolt disengaged, and we were punched in the face by a rush of stale air. He pushed the apartment door inward and flipped a few light switches on the wall just inside the jamb.

Not that such a thing was really possible anymore, or so I thought, but I felt sick to my stomach as I looked around the apartment as we made our way deeper into it. Vintage framed photographs were everywhere—hanging on the walls, propped up on tables—everywhere. Dietrich's family. His wife. His daughter. Some with just the daughter or the wife, some with both, and a few with all three of them. A morbid realization came over me.

"This was your place … is your place?"

"Yeah. It was rented out for many years, and then I had the chance to actually buy it about thirty years ago before the San Francisco real estate market went all stupid."

It was pretty personal and significant for Jonas to bring me here. I didn't think this was his actual resting place, his sanctuary. We both weren't ready for that yet, especially since mine had the bad habit of being found by my enemies.

"This isn't ..."

"Oh, God, no. Andrei knows this spot. I keep it for senti-mental reasons. I can't stand the thought of anyone else living here."

"So, this is where it happened?"

"Yeah."

"I'm sorry, Jonas, I really am."

He half huffed and half laughed at that. "Yeah, well. Have a seat, make yourself comfortable."

I parked myself on the couch while Jonas made his way to the kitchen. He pulled the refrigerator door open with one hand and pulled out two blood bags with the other. He tossed me one as he walked into the living room. He plopped on the couch next to me, trench coat and all. His manspreading was appreciable. He popped the top on his blood bag and sipped absentmindedly as he stared into the black mirror of a substantial flat screen television.

These things were far from satisfying but I figured I'd better. So, I obliged my host and tried to enjoy my *beverage* as best as I could.

"So."

"So."

"What were you able to pick up through the bat?"

I laid it out for him: Tim, the mercs, my brothers, Tobias, the Order of Ahura Mazda, all of it.

"It looks like they are using my parents' house as a base of operations and my brothers as bait. They have no idea that we planted a 'bug.' They don't know that we know."

Jonas turned his head in my direction.

"This is good news. We have the upper hand. I had a feeling there was more to Da Rocha."

"So, you didn't know about Ahura Mazda?"

"No, not at all. I always suspected something bigger, but they never showed themselves."

"Apparently, they thought Da Rocha was Billy Badass enough to handle me, you, and Andrei. They fucking thought wrong."

Jonas turned his head and resumed his vacant stare. "Yeah."

"What are we going to do, Jonas?"

"They have a lot of firepower, don't they?"

"Yeah, and they have no compunction using my family against me. They seem to think I am going to be stupid enough to return to my parents' house even after all this time. I have to honest, J, I have been tempted to seek my brothers out. Like a pull, a craving, a compulsion. The fact that they live out of state probably saved their lives, and the lives of their wives and kids. I still don't remember going to my parents' house that night, and I sure as fuck don't remember killing them. I just showed up there. What if I just show up there again?"

"When it was just Tim and the SWAT unit, I could just outmaneuver them. I could do things internally that threw Tim off my trail if I thought he was sniffing too close to me. Serge was a different animal, but he popped up at random, and I never did have a face-to-face with him like you did.

He had it bad for you. It brought the whole thing to a head. I don't agree with how we did it, but I have made my peace with the fact that he needed to go. But now we have brought the full weight of his organization down on top of our heads. When it was just SFPD, that was local, I always had the option of bugging out. Now, shit, Beth, this is world-wide. I don't know where the hell we can go."

I let the "Beth" slide this time. I'm not sure why.

"So, that's your solution? Run? Hide? I was trapped in a fucking coal mine for three days; I didn't like it too much. I don't know exactly where you think we can go." Remembering my Mary Shelley, I added, "I'm not prepared to go dogsledding across the arctic like some other monster I could mention."

"What do you propose? If we fight, the odds are not stacked in our favor. The two of us against heavily armed paramilitary types who know who and what we are?"

"Well, there could be five …"

"What?!?! Get the … are you serious?"

"He helped us with Da Rocha. He could be convinced to join us for this. It would be in his best interest to see Tobias and Ahura Mazda wiped out."

"What kind of Satanic *Fellowship of the Ring* kind of bull-shit are you proposing?"

"Well, there would be me, you, Andrei, Julie, and Sarah."

"I got that."

I sidled next to Jonas until our thighs were touching.

Our shoulders bumped as he turned his head in my direction again. I leaned in and kissed him full on the mouth. His lips were soft and sweet. The tips of our tongues met, and I gently broke the kiss.

"Trust me."

CHAPTER XV

Jonas was kind enough to offer his emergency sanctuary to me. Basically it was his old bedroom, the one he had shared with his wife, but it had been day-proofed. The furniture was vintage, hell, it was probably original. Heavy oak dressers and matching bed frame, bedclothes the likes of which I had only seen in movies. More photos. Blackout curtains were duct-taped to the wall, threatening to ruin the 1940's aesthetic. I settled in as daybreak approached.

"What about you?"

"Don't worry about me. I'll be back shortly after sundown."

"Promise?"

"Promise."

After Jonas closed the door behind him and placed what

I assumed was a towel under the door, I buried myself under the covers of the bed and cocooned myself. I had a lot on my mind. Our surveillance operation had yielded much. Running and hiding just wasn't an option. I wished it were. But if Ahura Mazda was as well-funded and well-equipped as I thought it was, we'd be found and exterminated eventually. Survival was the only thing. As misbegotten as this existence was, I had grown to enjoy continuing to live, if you could call it living.

I had a few ideas on how we could emerge victorious. I definitely knew how we were going to get SFPD off our backs. I had Tim's address; I'd gotten it from his office at the police station. I knew his name, his wife's name, and I'd learned they had a child.

As for Ahura Mazda, I had some thoughts there too, but they weren't fully formed. I needed more information about the Order. Was Tobias the main guy? Where were they headquartered? How many religious organizations did they reach into with their tentacles? How many people was I going to have to kill? Would I survive? Would Andrei and his harem join up? Would they survive? Would I care if they didn't?

What I did know was that I had more than just Jonas on my side and possibly Andrei, Sarah, and Julie to conscript. I had the children of the night at my disposal, and I could sense their anticipation rising as I slipped off into my preternatural sleep. I could have sworn I heard Blackfoot caterwauling out on Jones Street.

I awoke a little bit after sunset. Fumbling around in the darkness of the unfamiliar, it took me a few moments to remember where I was and to orient myself to the surroundings. That just proved the effectiveness of the blackout conditions Jonas had created. Even my eyes needed a moment to adjust.

The bedroom was typical—queen-size bed, chest of drawers, dresser, and nightstands flanking the bed. Everything was heavy oak. A wallet, a watch with a leather band, and a gold band wedding ring sat on top of the chest of drawers. The dresser was covered with a lady's things. A hairbrush, makeup, a powder puff box ... the only thing that was missing was the large mirror one might find mounted to the back of the dresser.

Jonas had yet to return, so I took it upon myself to do some exploring. The apartment was furnished straight out of the 1940s. Ornate tiered end tables framed the couch where the two of us had sat and conspired just a few hours earlier. The kitchen featured a very small but quaint banquette. I took a peek in the fridge and found another blood bag. Since I didn't know when I would be able to hunt again, I figured what the hell? I popped the top and sipped from the rubbery plastic pouch while I wandered around the surprisingly spacious flat. Everything was as it was when Jonas had been alive. The photos captured happy times, loving times. I half expected the Missus to emerge from the bathroom after a freshening up.

I'm ashamed to admit that I jumped a bit when I heard

the key inserted into the lock. A look of surprise came over Jonas's face as he entered and saw me standing there sipping some chilled O+.

"I see you raided the fridge."

"I didn't think you'd mind, especially since you probably wouldn't want me snacking on your neighbors."

This drew a hearty laugh from the detective.

"You loved them quite a bit, didn't you?" I tossed my head at a particularly large clump of framed photos arranged on an end table.

"Very much." His voice trailed off.

He tugged off the rucksack that had been slung over his shoulder and restocked the fridge with more blood bags.

"I know they're no substitute for the real thing, but as you said, it beats snacking on the neighbors."

"If you say so, detective. I'm going to pay Tim a visit."

"Why?"

"Don't ask questions you don't want the answers to, Jonas."

"C'mon, Elizabeth, he's a good cop, a good *man*."

I'm not sure Jonas knew what misogyny was, but the recently minted demonic feminist in me took exception to his calling Tim a good *man*.

"Look, Jonas. There is only us and them now. HuMANS are the enemy. I don't care how you felt about them then. You did what you had to do to blend in, to get along. This is now, you have to do what you need to do NOW."

"I know, I get it, but …"

"No ifs, ands, or buts. We need to work our way up the food chain if we are ever going to get these fools off our back. And it starts with your pal. Back in a jiff, don't wait up."

It was a short flight to Noe Valley. For the life of me I didn't understand how a San Francisco PD cop could afford to live here. Jonas's apartment made some kind of sense. He'd bought it before the market exploded. But these houses here in Noe Valley were seven-figure homes. I never did get the impression that Lieutenant Tim Prentice was a dirty cop, so maybe his wife made bank. What was her name? Oh, yeah. Kelsi. I had a little trouble finding Carnelian Way. It was nestled between Diamond Heights Boulevard and Clipper Street. It snaked from Duncan Street to Douglass Park. I flew over the dog park and approached from the south, landing on the roof and transforming in one continuous roll.

I hovered outside the window on the Carnelian side. That was the nice thing about this time of year, the sun went down early. And I really liked people who didn't lock their windows.

This particular condo had three bedrooms and three bathrooms. The baby's room faced Carnelian. A strategic mistake. I wasn't a mom, I didn't have kids, I was never going to have kids, and even I knew you didn't have the baby's room face the street. And I damn sure knew you didn't leave the window unlocked.

There was enough of a gap in the curtains for me to

spy Kelsi putting a toddler in her crib. I waited for the lieutenant's wife to leave the room before I tried the window. It slid open with ease. Maybe it was my unnatural strength, maybe it was the quality of the window, maybe it was both. Whatever it was, I was in the baby's room lickety-split. I sat in the rocking chair in the corner for a long while contemplating my options. What to do, what to do.

The child, north of a year old but not quite two, cooed in her crib. The room was typical for a girl child with stereotypical white heterosexual parents. What I mean to say is, it was fucking pink. Disgustingly so. Everything was a lousy shade of pink. The walls, the ceiling, the dresser, the crib, even the fucking diaper genie was pink. Of course they had a diaper genie.

Tim was working, most likely. The question was, on what, exactly? Was he with Tobias and the armed overgrown muscle heads of Ahura Mazda plotting my demise, or was he doing his actual job solving the murders and robberies of the humans of San Francisco? It didn't really matter, did it?

I took the little one for a walk in the park.

She was a cute thing with rosy round cheeks and a pouty mouth. I wiped the salty tears away as I sat with her on a bench across the way from the Prentices' residence. The toddler looked up at me with tear-filled eyes and repeated, "Mama."

"Shhhh. I'm not going to hurt you, sweetie-pie."

That was a little white lie. I wasn't going to hurt her ... much.

I grabbed her by the wrist and pulled back the fabric of her pajamas. My fangs penetrated the soft, young flesh easily. I didn't bite down deep enough to puncture the veins, just a few capillaries to draw some sweet nectar. As I withdrew from the child's arm, I licked my lips and devoured what little blood I did draw. It made me shiver.

By the time her mother thought to look for her, little Daphne ... yes, her fucking name was Daphne ... was sitting in a pile of leaves under a tree, blood was trickling from her wrist, and she was sobbing. Daphne—I knew her name was Daphne because her mother wouldn't stop screaming it—was just fine. I had harmed enough young people for an eternity, and I wasn't going to do it again. This was just to get her mother's attention and freak her out a little.

For a young woman, Kelsi was bedtime frumpy. Flannel pajamas, a housecoat, and thick cozy slippers—all she was missing was a colorful, clarifying face mask. I slipped back into the townhouse before Kelsi could return with her mewling daughter.

The now doting mother took Daphne into the bathroom to clean the blood from her wrist.

"Oh, baby girl, how did you get outside? What happened, honey? Did something scratch you?"

Daphne shook her head "no."

"Did something bite you?"

Daphne nodded her head "yes."

"Oh, honey."

After cleaning the little girl up and dressing her wound, Kelsi put her in fresh pajamas and took her back to her room. The little girl settled in without protest. Her mother covered her up with a blanket and kissed her on the forehead.

"Goodnight, sweetie."

"Mama … M-mm-m-mama."

Kelsi turned on a heel and headed back toward her daughter's bedroom door only to find me in the doorway.

"Hello, Kelsi."

My face, with her precious little one's blood smeared on my lips, was the last thing she ever saw.

CHAPTER XVI

I t was just past four o'clock in the morning when I heard the key inserted into the lock and the deadbolt disengage. Tim Prentice entered his home in total darkness like he always did. He made his way to the kitchen and put his keys in a candy dish on the counter like he always did. He took his sport coat off and hung it up on the coat rack in the hall like he always did. He removed his service weapon and locked it in the gun safe in the front hall closet like he always did. He removed his shoulder holster and hung it up with his jacket like he always did. He made his way to the refrigerator for a beer and a snack like he always did.

He tripped over his wife's dead body, landed in a lake of blood on the kitchen floor, and lost consciousness when his head hit the granite countertop.

While I was waiting for Tim to get home, I had plenty of time to rummage through drawers and cupboards. When he came around he was zip-tied to a chair while wearing nothing but his t-shirt, his boxer shorts, and his dress socks. I sat across from him, straddling a backward dining chair like I was the detective interrogating a suspect.

"Bright red? Impressive sock game."

"Fuck you." He didn't so much say it, he spat it.

"Shhhh, detective. You'll wake your daughter."

"I swear to God, if you've hurt her."

"You'll do what?"

Through gritted teeth, "I'll kill you."

I chuckled at this, which seemed to make him angrier.

"Go ahead, get mad. It makes the blood richer, hotter. I would ask you where all of your case files were, all your notes on me and Jonas and Andrei and Ahura Mazda, but I already found them."

I tapped a large leather case with the side of my foot.

"So now what? You going to bite me?"

"Like I bit your daughter?"

Tim struggled and tugged at his restraints. His efforts were in vain.

"I like a man who is old school, a little old-fashioned too. You come across as the modern, new age whatever-the-fuck, but you have some interesting sensibilities."

I pulled out the straight razor I'd found in the bathroom and extended the blade.

"This is nice. You actually shave with this thing? I

couldn't imagine trying to shave my legs with it. But then again, I don't have to anymore, now, do I?"

"Look, bitch, you killed my wife, and when I get free I'm going to kill you."

I was starting to understand why Andrei didn't care for foul language. Not that I was ever going to change the way I talked, but it did seem to be a common refrain from "food."

Tim tried to turn his head like an owl to see where I was going as I maneuvered behind him. There was no way in hell I was going to bite him. I wasn't going to give him the satisfaction. I ran my fingers through his hair, grabbed a fistful with my off hand, and yanked his head back. I slit his throat with the straight razor.

It was strange. I fed from him but I didn't enjoy it. No bloodlust orgasmic experience. No nothing. The blood gave me restorative energy but no shudder, no electrification of my loins. Figures.

Before I stole off into the night, I walked back into Daphne's room and took her by the ankle. I dragged a sharp nail across the bottom of her foot. She mumbled, "Mama, mmmm, Mmmama," in her sleep. I scooped up the satchel and headed out. I was back at my sanctuary before sunrise, but I didn't have any time to go over the contents of the bag. Dietrich was going to have to wait as well. He was going to find out the hard way what I'd done. I really didn't care. I looked at it as working my way up the food chain. Eventually I'd get to Tobias or his superiors, if he had any. Or they'd take me out first.

When I woke, I immediately began poring over Tim's case file and notes. As I suspected, that wasn't the first meeting between the newly departed Tim Prentice and representatives of the Order of Ahura Mazda. A snigger escaped every time I thought Ahura Mazda, I couldn't help but think about the car manufacturer.

The more I read, the more I came to understand that the SFPD had a public relations mess on their hands. Law enforcement professionals end up with egg on their face when multiple serial killers cause hate and discontent all over their jurisdiction. Dietrich had done a great job of covering his tracks over the years. He was able to pursue Andrei and keep his real identity a secret for decades. I was the anomaly. I was the fly in the ointment. My creation turned the whole thing upside-down. My lack of self-control and self-discipline brought unwanted attention and drew Da Rocha, and eventually his comrades, out. Funny. It was Dietrich's lack of self-control that really exposed the under-belly of this sordid affair.

If I played my cards right, I would be able to eliminate Ahura Mazda and Andrei in one fell swoop and live in peace for a while. I was not naive enough to believe that would be the end of it. There would always be cops or clergy or military or secret societies or Frog brothers. But just as Serge Da Rocha had been, this was an immediate threat.

Hopefully Dietrich had made himself useful and done some research on the mercenaries who were trying to end us. Somehow I doubted that; I figured he had just spent the time waiting for me. I found him in his old apartment sitting in the dark in the living room. He didn't hear me coming.

"You did a good job keeping this piece of real estate a secret. I'm shocked Tobias and his goons aren't crawling all over it by now."

"Liz! Oh, shit, you startled me."

"Yeah, well, not an easy thing to do, I suppose."

"How the heck did you get in here?"

"You really shouldn't leave the bedroom window open, especially at night. You know what might fly in."

"No kidding. So, I'd ask what you've been up to since we parted company, but it's all over the news. Tim was a good cop, a good guy too, and Kelsi … well, did you hav-"

"Look, I, *we* needed to send a message to Tobias and his goons. We are not to be trifled with. He needs to know that he can be gotten at any time."

"Don't you think his guard will be up even more so now?"

"If that's the case, then he isn't worth his salt, now, is he?"

"So, now what?"

"We contact Andrei and his little harem. With any luck, they'll want to team up and end this as badly as we do."

"How do you suppose we do that?"

"Leave that to me."

We hopped in the Accent that I was shocked hadn't

been impounded yet and headed for Golden Gate Park. Before long, we were parked and walking toward the little pond where we'd had our Come-to-Jesus meeting after dispatching Da Rocha. I thought it was fitting. I sat on a large boulder and drew pictographs in the sand along the water's edge while Jonas paced.

"This isn't going to work."

"Shhhh, Jonas, of course it is. Trust me."

I reached out with my mind, with my feelings … keep your *Star Wars* clichés to yourself … concentrating with my considerable might. Heavy, dark clouds rolled in, and somewhere in the distance thunder rumbled. My emotions had brought forth storms before but this was different. I was summoning. The connection to Andrei had always been one of anger and the desire for revenge. I wasn't dumb enough to think that he didn't have some sort of tether to his progeny. The funny thing was, somehow, Sarah was mine.

I envisioned my psychic tendrils encircling all three of them and drawing them to this very spot. It took longer than I thought. By the time I opened my eyes, Dietrich's jaw had dropped.

"B-b-b-uh, y-y-y …"

"Spit it out, Jonas,"

"You're floating."

Floating wasn't the right word for it. I was levitating. I looked down and saw that I was a good four feet above the rock I had been sitting on. As Andrei's fog bank rolled in, my body drifted back down to my perch. He materialized out of nothing. Within minutes, Sarah and Julie approached from opposite directions.

"Well, well, well, isn't this a pleasant surprise. How are you, Miss Elizabeth?"

Andrei's attempts at charm always came across as smarmy, and this was no different.

"Yes, hello, Elizabeth, can't say I'm pleased to see you." Sarah wasn't good at hiding her bitterness.

"Liz!" I couldn't tell if Julie was genuinely happy to see me or if she was being facetious.

Dietrich stepped out from the shadows in plain view of everyone. Only Andrei acknowledged him.

"Detective."

"Andrei," Jonas said through clenched teeth.

"Pull up a rock, everyone."

Andrei, Julie, Sarah, and Jonas each found a suitable place to sit. Part of me felt like I was back in a conference room about to give an advertising pitch to a client. An even bigger part of me was wondering why I was in charge of what I hoped to be a little vampire hit squad.

"*We* have a problem."

"Who's this 'we,' Elizabeth? I'm doing just fine."

"Oh, really, Sarah? That's why you're running around the Bay stealing babies. Yeah, you're just fine."

Sarah hung her head and cast her eyes downward. Funny, I half expected to see her reflection in the pond. "Thought so."

"What is this all about, Liz?"

"Well, Jules, there's a secret society of vampire hunters stalking me and Jonas, and more than likely the three of you." I nodded in Andrei's general direction.

"Just who exactly, *kincsem?*"

"Do I really have to spell it out, Andrei? Are you familiar with the Order of the Ahura Mazda? That's where our friend Da Rocha came from."

"Who or what the hell is a Mazda RX-8, or whatever?"

"Crack a book, Jules. Look, this team of paramilitary yo-yos is using my parents' house as a base, and my brothers are the bait."

"Who's in charge?"

"Why do I have a feeling you already know? A guy named Tobias."

Andrei sucked air into his mouth and through his teeth. It sounded like someone was filling up a basketball.

"So, you do know, you are familiar."

I laid it all out for them. I told them everything I knew, everything I had observed through the bumblebee bat, all that Jonas and I had discussed and theorized. I told them about Tim and his wife. I proposed a plan of action.

"Are you out of your fucking mind, Elizabeth?"

"No, Sarah, I am not. This is the only way. You all have access to information or have skills that can help. If we don't get ahead of this, if we don't take them out, they will hunt us down. I don't know about you all, but I have grown fond of this existence. It's better than no existence. Wouldn't you agree?"

After a long moment of furtive glances and kicking rocks …

"I take it from your silence that I have my answer."

"I do so under protest."

"I really don't give a shit, Sarah. We don't know how long they're going to hole up at my parents' house, and I'd rather move now while we know where they are. Get the information I asked you to get, by any means necessary, and meet me at Coit Tower tomorrow night just after sundown."

"It's only open until six o'clock."

Julie wilted under the heat of my glare. "Anyone else?"

My merry little band of vampire hunter slayers started to break up and drift off. Well, I wasn't sure what the hell Dietrich was doing since he was kinda with me.

"Andrei, a word?"

"Yes, *kincsem?*"

"What the hell does that mean, what is that … Hungarian?"

"I underestimate you, my dear."

"You have since the very beginning. Let's go for a walk."

He offered his arm. I refused to take it. Dietrich called after us. "Elizabeth?!?"

"I'll be back, Jonas. Don't worry. He can't do anything to me he hasn't done already."

A sly smile curled Andrei's lips.

"Don't get any ideas, ass."

We walked along a path for a good while in silence. My thoughts drifted to previous adventures in Golden Gate Park —the bongo player, the cops, the lovers, becoming a wolf, tangling with a hawk—good times.

"How did you avoid them all these years, Andrei?"

"Until you came along, I … how you say … um … flew under the … what is word?"

"Radar?"

"Yes, that's it. I kept to myself, I didn't turn anyone … that often. I stayed in the shadows. Unlike you, I don't feed very often."

"How old are you, really?"

"Oh, I don't see how or why that is important."

"HOW OLD?!?!"

"I am four hundred and ninety-three years old."

I stopped in my tracks. After a few steps, Andrei turned and walked back to me. When our eyes met the reality of my existence finally sank in. I was going to live forever. People I knew and loved would wither and die, and I would go on. I would never fall in love. I would never marry. I would never have children. Some of these things I knew and had somewhat made my peace with, but the longevity, the endlessness of it all was like a shovel to the face.

"I know exactly how you feel."

A steely resolve swelled in my belly, traveled up and caught in my throat. I liked being alive. And I was pretty sure I liked this better. I had been dead once. Now, I was fairly certain that my conscious state during rigor mortis was a byproduct of the turning or the becoming or whatever you wanted to call it, but I damn sure didn't care for it. Maybe there was an afterlife, but I hadn't seen it, I hadn't experienced it. Neither heaven or hell called for me. If this was purgatory or the pleroma, it sure looked like the San Francisco Bay Area. That being the case, I didn't like what was on the other side of death. I preferred to bring death. I was death.

"I have encountered Tobias twice before. He is a formidable foe. He has dispatched many of our kind."

"Why didn't you take him out?"

"Self-preservation was more important at the time. But now, things and the stakes have changed. Never have there been so many of us here in San Francisco at one time. And your penchant for attracting unwanted attention has the Order of Ahura Mazda on a mission to stamp us out."

"Oh, sure, blame me."

I lit a cigarette and blew the smoke in Andrei's face. His faux cough almost made me laugh, but then I remembered how much I hated him. And I hated myself for needing him right now ... again. But I couldn't see any other way out of this mess. There was nowhere to go, nowhere to hide. If I tried to run, Tobias and his goons would find me. To me, the only option was to take on the Order of Ahura Mazda, and I hoped they were a small, tight-knit organization, not some international cabal.

"What do you think of my plan?"

"I think it could work. It has to."

"You're not going to disappear are you? You're not going to bail on us?"

"No. As much as I'd like to vanish into the fog, I agree with you that Ahura Mazda must be dealt with. Especially now."

I did take Andrei's arm for the walk back to the pond. Not to worry, no Stockholm syndrome here, I just wanted to feel something solid, something real, as ludicrous as that may sound. As we approached the little body of water that was shrouded by trees and large rocks, Jonas stepped out from behind a shrubbery.

Andrei's elbow that had borne the weight of my arm dissipated and my limb fell to my side. I turned, only to see a large cloud of mist, which quickly vanished on the evening wind. I just hoped he would keep his word.

"Well?"

"Well, what, Jonas?"

"What was that all about?

"Never you mind. Jealous?"

"Maybe."

"Let's go. I'll drive. We can just make it."

This was one of those occasions when I wished Jonas could transform into something that could fly. But we had to make do. I willed the Accent as fast as I dared and raced to Montgomery Street. We dumped the car in the first parking spot I could find.

"C'mon!"

I grabbed Jonas by the hand, and we took off running for Pier 33. Traffic was heavy on the Embarcadero but we won our game of Frogger and just did make the last ferry to Alcatraz. We found a seat and settled in. The water was rough and tossed the boat. The rocking was unnerving and reminded me of my experience at Drawbridge in the creek or the river or whatever it was. Running water was not my friend, and neither were the dark blue-purple white-capped waves of the San Francisco Bay. The fifteen-minute ride to prison-turned-tourist-attraction felt like three weeks.

The look I gave the attendant froze his blood and glassed his eyes. Turns out Jonas and I didn't need tickets after all. I rested my head on his shoulder and gritted my teeth for the duration.

We waited until the tourists disembarked from the ferry before we followed suit. Jonas and I blended in with the tail end of a large group, then walked past the ranger station on the left and the guard tower on the right. We bypassed the audio tour device pickup, followed the tourists into the cell house, and made our way around. The last ferry wasn't until 9:25 p.m., so we had plenty of time to kill. It was fun dodging park rangers and docents as we took our own private tour of this historic landmark.

"You remember when it was a prison, don't you?" I asked as we made our way outside to the recreation yard.

"I sure do. Sent a few guys here too."

We climbed over the wall and found a place to sit on the west side of Alcatraz Island.

"I remember the Native American occupation too. They held it for a year and a half. You weren't even born yet. The 1960s were a crazy time here. The Free Speech Movement in Berkeley, the Black Panthers in Oakland, the Vietnam war protests, hippies, The Haight, what a time."

"What was Alcatraz like when it was in use?"

"It was brutal. I almost felt sorry for some of them. The audio tour tells it better than I can, but the cons had to listen to New Year's Eve revelers across the Bay. It was torture."

"Do you believe the stories about the escape? The three men they never found, I mean."

"You know something, I think I do. I think they got away. It was in use as a prison for less than a year after that."

I had watched a documentary about it once. In 1962, John and Clarence Anglin and Frank Morris pulled off the impossible; they did what people said could never be done. They got off of "The Rock." I was starting to think taking on Tobias and the Order of Ahura Mazda was an impossible feat.

"Here we are again, Jonas. Teaming up to take an enemy down. This time it isn't just one guy, it's a whole bunch of guys."

"Yeah. Part of me thinks you're nuts. The other part knows this has to be done. You know I don't care for this kind of thing. Even if we split up, go our separate ways, we'll be hunted down and destroyed. So, I'm all in."

A cold late fall wind picked up and blew through Jonas's hair. His trench coat blew open like a cloak. I felt the coming winter chill but it didn't bother me. It was rather soothing. The waning gibbous moon was at our backs and any moonlight was weak and blocked by prison structures. We watched the dark blue waves crash against the edge of the island, and I wondered what it would have been like to have been imprisoned here.

I slept in a coffin, for fuck's sake.

I wrapped my arm around Jonas's, and he enveloped me in his trench coat. We sat in silence like this for a long while as we waited for the last of the tourists and park employees to call it a night. This was the earliest I had retired to my main sanctuary since I'd taken up residence, so I wanted to make sure the place was good and deserted.

My mind was restless but my body wasn't, and I was perfectly content waiting out the staff hooked to my good detective's arm like a barnacle. It was past eleven o'clock when I decided it would be safe to retire for the night. That was one of the other advantages of being undead—not showing up on surveillance cameras.

I stood up, took Jonas by the hand, and led him to my makeshift crypt. Fallen, crumbled slabs of rock hid the crevice that led to an old crawlspace and maintenance closet. We made our way through, climbing over chunks of concrete until the crawlspace opened into a void. An old cistern sat in the middle. I took out my lighter and lit a few candles that I had placed in strategic locations. A circular stone slab covered the cistern.

"It's not high-gloss mahogany with a velvet interior, but it does the trick."

"I must admit, Elizabeth, very creative. I'm not sure how you came up with this idea but it's pretty ingenious. I don't even want to know how you found this space. What's interesting is that instead of teardown and rebuild, they just kept building on top of the original structure."

"Oh, shut up, will you?"

I flew to Jonas, pulled his trench coat down pinning his arms, and kissed him full on the mouth. My serpentine tongue forced his mouth open and found his. We undressed each other fast and rough. And then kissed and caressed slow and gentle.

We made love right there on the stone lid. I hadn't thought I would ever have traditional sex again, but I was gladly mistaken. It hurt when he entered me. It was a tearing, a gentle ripping sensation. But the pain subsided as he repeated his pelvic thrusts.

I didn't climax, not that I ever could that way. But the experience was enjoyable nonetheless. Jonas was a sweet, experienced lover. It felt good to have him between my legs, his weight on top of me. There was no biting, although I doubted vampire blood would have done either one of us any good. Just like I knew sunlight, running water, and crosses were bad for my health, I kinda knew that another vampire's blood would have no nutritional value. As we lay there in the concrete, I wondered how Jonas had gotten and maintained an erection. It really wasn't important.

Jonas was on his back, my head rested on his chest, and my arm and leg were draped over his midsection. I had taken to sealing myself up in the cistern with the stone cap covering the opening. The bottom of the cistern was filled in with dirt and debris. It made for an adequate makeshift grave.

"Are you staying?"

"It's a few hours before sunup, and I do have my assignment. I think I'll go back to the apartment and do my research."

"How are you go-"

He put his finger to my lips. "Shhhhh. Don't worry your pretty little head."

Jonas slid from beneath my head, arm, and leg and gathered his clothes. I watched him get dressed with great interest. It had been a long time since I had observed this ritual. There weren't many men in my life whose movements fascinated me or held my interest. Maybe I just wanted to see how a vampire got dressed.

"I put my pants on one leg at a time, like everyone else."

A hearty laugh escaped my throat, and the sound echoed off the walls of the chamber. Embarrassed that I was caught watching, I covered my mouth with my hand like a schoolgirl, and my laugh turned into a high-pitched giggle.

"I'll see you at Coit Tower tonight."

"K." I bit my lip and tried to put on a smolder, but Jonas never looked back. Instead he exited the way we'd come in, through the maintenance closet and crawlspace out into the dank night air of the converted prison. I threw something on and blew out the candles before climbing into the cistern and sliding the lid into place. A grin of satisfaction graced my face before the catatonic state came and took me.

CHAPTER XVII

When I awoke, I slid the heavy stone lid aside just enough for egress. The grinding of the concrete made such a racket. I didn't need the ranger or Yogi and Boo-Boo to get curious and go all Indiana Jones looking for the source of the noise. I lit a few candles. Not that I really needed them; call them creature comforts.

As I dressed, I felt something brush my legs. When I looked down I was stunned to find Blackfoot making figure eights, as she was wont to do. "How in the bloody hell did you find your way here, you lunatic cat? Never mind, don't answer that, I don't want to know." I scooped Blackfoot up into my arms and sat on the edge of the cistern. She relaxed and started kneading my knees with her paws and sharp claws. I scratched her between her ears and under her chin, and stroked the fur along the length of her body. I picked out the few burrs I felt. One must have hurt as I extracted it, because she made a sound I had never heard before and bit my hand.

"Sorry, just trying to help, you little bitch."

Blackfoot found a corner to crawl into as I wondered how long it would be before more nocturnal castaways would find my lair as they had with the abandoned church. Oh, sure, there were a few rats, mice, and spiders, but I think they were already in residence long before I arrived. I finished getting ready, blew out the candles, and made my way out into the cell house. Not that it would be unusual for a bat to be seen flying over Alcatraz Island, but I don't think the tourists would have quite grasped watching me transform into one. Besides, I didn't mind the ferry. Just like the BART train, I liked the trappings of human existence, once in a while … once in a great while.

After I set foot on terra firma, I crossed The Embarcadero and made my way to the last known parking spot of the Hyundai Accent. Of course, it wasn't there. Aside from floating on occasion, it didn't seem like Jonas had any other abilities or powers. Well, vampire talents anyway. I found a shady spot, transformed, and flew off to Coit Tower.

I flew through one of the arched openings and found that I was the second to arrive. Jonas was already there, sitting on a railing.

"Hello, lover."

"Good evening, Elizabeth. How'd you sleep?"

"Just fine."

"Are we interrupting something?"

A ding from the elevator bank signaled Sarah's and Julie's arrival.

"Been waiting long, Elizabeth?"

"No, Sarah. I just got here."

"And I've been here for a while."

Julie and Sarah exchanged knowing glances. I didn't think it was that obvious that Jonas and I had slept together.

Of course, Andrei was fashionably late. Julie was the most impatient of us, shifting her weight from leg to leg, gnawing on her thumb, tapping her foot. Sarah paced a little, wandered a little, and sneered a lot. Jonas just sat on his railing.

After what seemed like an hour, a cloud of foggy mist rolled and ebbed toward us, filling numerous archways at once. Andrei, impeccably dressed in his trademark tailored black suit and crisp, white dress shirt, stepped out of the cloud. One too many buttons were undone on that shirt, adding to his smarmy quality.

"Jesus Christ, Andrei, seriously?"

Mr. Dramatic Entrance didn't say anything, he just smiled at me. Had I real blood in my veins, it would have curdled. Strange bedfellows, my ass. This would be our last meeting like this. We were going to have to find an out of the way spot for our confabs. I was hoping we wouldn't need many more.

"Okay, people, what have we got?"

Sarah started. "Your guy, what's his name …?"

"Tobias?"

"Yeah, that's him. Anyway, he left your parents' house just one time. He went to this little coffee shop on South J Street. He actually walked. I mean, who does that? He knows what he's hunting."

"Was he alone or did he go with his guard dogs?"

"I didn't see any dogs. But yeah, he went by himself. Well, no, that isn't right. A couple of his guys tagged along, but they were hanging back, giving him his space. He sat in the cafe until they closed. He had a few shots of espresso and a pastry."

I wasn't sure if this was something we could use to our advantage. Was this a habit or a one-time thing? He couldn't get one of my sisters-in-law to make him a coffee?

"Did he stop anywhere along the way?"

"You know what? Yeah, he did. He stood under this tree for a long while, it was like he was sniffing the air."

Jonas and I made eye contact. It wasn't a good thing.

"Jules?"

"They rotate personnel, probably more than I thought they would. Technicians kept coming and going so I never could get an accurate count of how many were in the house at any given time. But two of the big guys left at four in the morning. They hadn't returned by the time I had to, you know, retire. They don't flinch or blink when Tobias is around. There's always someone in the support vehicles. One of them looks like it has a satellite link up, and another has like this parabolic antenna on it, for sound, I think."

"What about my family?"

"I could only see them through the windows; not once did they come outside, not even for a smoke or a breath of fresh air."

A picture was starting to come into view. It might be possible to take out the techs who were surveilling the house, hell, we might be able to get to Tobias if he did indeed have a nightly espresso habit, but a prolonged siege with military types would destroy the house, kill or injure my brothers and their wives, and most certainly attract Livermore law enforcement. But maybe we could draw them out.

"I need to know where those two goons go at four a.m., and I need to know if it's the same two every time. So we're going to need another night or two. Sarah? Is there anyone you can trust that could follow them during daylight hours?"

"I might, I dunno, yeah, maybe. Oh, hell, do I have to? Don't make me call him … "

"Sarah, we need this information. Please?"

She nodded her approval, but she really didn't want to.

"Jonas?"

"So, Tim's murder has been swept under the rug. The Order has some serious clout. It's not on the news or the web, and he's listed as 'on vacation' on the duty roster. His little one is with Child Protective Services."

"How the hell do you know that?"

"You don't want to know."

"This is good news. This means the only agency we have to deal with here is Ahura Mazda, no SFPD, no FBI."

"This makes total sense. The Order doesn't want any interference; they don't want any other organizations mucking things up, so they arrange for a wide berth so they can have the latitude to take us down without causing a panic."

"Andrei?"

"There is truth to what the detective says. Our new friend Tobias appears to have been contacted and contracted by the Archdiocese of San Francisco. Da Rocha was supposed to diffuse the situation but, as we all know, he failed. What I find fascinating is Tobias's belief in the old trope that you will go home again. Especially after so much time has passed. You have already, no? Perhaps this is why your brothers are being used. As we suspected, they are bait."

We were batting .500 on the information front. Sarah and Julie needed to go back to Livermore and get a bit more intel. I wasn't sure what to do with Andrei and Jonas, or what I wanted them to do until then. Well, I had an idea about what to do with one of them, but that wasn't important right now. They both assured me they had plenty to do.

I was getting thirsty.

This was the first time I had awakened after a night of not feeding when I didn't feel like I was going to end up slaughtering a bunch of people. Maybe it was the thrill of the operation at hand. Maybe it was the fact that I had gotten laid for the first time in forever. Maybe the thirst was starting to abate over time like it had with Andrei. Whatever it was, I was glad about it, but I also knew it wasn't going to last.

"Let's meet back here at five a.m. We'll compare notes and set the battle plan."

Our merry band of vampire outlaws nodded their approval, and we split up for the night, each with an important assignment. The girls headed out via the elevator with Dietrich, Andrei poofed through an archway, and I transformed into a bat and took wing.

I flew off looking for a shady spot to sit and think. It ended up becoming a pleasure flight. I banked right and headed southeast along the Embarcadero and then took a sharp left and vectored northeast along I-80 and the Bay Bridge. I flapped up to a comfortable altitude high above the glare of the car headlights and where I couldn't see the water. Making a slight left, I made a circuit around Yerba Buena and Treasure Island before getting back on course for the East Bay.

As I approached Emeryville, I made a sharp right turn and headed south. After circling Alameda Point and the old Naval Air Station Alameda, I made my way north. Before long I was at César E. Chávez Park on the very edge of Berkeley. I landed near a structure reminiscent of Stonehenge and transformed. I walked along the Dorothy Stegmann trail between the tiny Stonehenge and the ocean. The waves lapped gently against the land. There was a good spit between me and the water, and that kept me from freaking about being close to it. The Alcatraz ferry ride was bad enough even though I had chosen it. I didn't need any more self-induced dread.

The sky was clear, dark, black, and purple all at the same time. Karl the Fog had taken the night off, it seemed. The air was cool and crisp. The onset of winter was on the horizon. I really didn't care. Normally this park was full of kite flyers and picnickers, but tonight the only visitor was a lonely vampire contemplating the possible end of her existence.

I found a large rock to curl up on. Since I was the Queen of Random Thoughts, my mind was full of them as if I had wandered onto the Bay Bridge and walked into oncoming traffic. Images and concepts flew by like speeding cars on the freeway. Horns blared, but they really weren't automobiles and irate drivers, they were my own memories and premonitions all congealed in this big Gordian knot. If I could just find the right end to yank, the solutions to all my problems would roll out in front of me.

There was Tobias and Ahura Mazda, my brothers and their wives, the SFPD and God knows what other law enforcement agencies, the news media, the boutique, stealing from Best Buy and Anthropologie, the guy from Taco Bell, the ménage à trois guys, the vampire twins Tweedle Dee and Tweedle Dum, Serge Da Rocha and ... and ... and of course Dietrich, dear sweet Dietrich.

The jumble calmed down when I could focus my

thoughts on my hard-boiled detective. After the night we'd spent together, I felt closer to him more than ever. I felt like I could trust him, more than I could before. So many times I had wanted to get near him, understand him, *know* him. But he was aloof and detached, wrapped up in his pursuit of Andrei. He'd saved my bacon back at Land's End, and for that I would be eternally grateful. But he'd sure let me down in the fight against Da Rocha.

I don't think I was ever going to understand his hesitation that night. I hadn't exactly let him help me against Andrei that night Julie had died. I was going to take that rat bastard out myself. There was nothing Jonas could do. Did he hesitate that night too? Or did things just happen so fast that he didn't have a chance to react?

I replayed all of our encounters on the big screen in my head. From the moment I became aware of his existence in the world to Whitney's murder and everything in between. That night Billy and I had called him to try to get him to bust Andrei. His restaurateur friends, the one good and the other not so good. Christina. Mmmmm. Was she delicious or what? Bad timing and bad choice of venue, but I just couldn't resist her.

And that led me back to Jonas.

I didn't know if I would ever have sex with him again. I definitely wanted to. But if things went sideways, if our little commando operation went askew, well, this little romance was going to end before it ever really got started.

He seemed committed to the task at hand. His hesitation

had given way to following instructions. He was back to being the Jonas Dietrich I thought he was when I first started tailing him and trying to get close to him. And I liked that. I liked it quite a bit.

I rocked back and forth on my rock, my knees together, and made yummy, cooing sounds as I thought about that night with Jonas—how warm he was between my legs, how expertly he touched me, the strength and passion in his kisses. Mmmmmm. I wanted him again.

"Am I interrupting something?"

"Sarah?!?" I just about fell off my rock. "What the fuck are you doing here?"

"I followed you. Alameda Point is hopping tonight, you should have put in there for a ... bite." Fuck, I forgot she could transform into a bat.

She bit her lower lip and dragged her toe through the gravel as "bite" escaped her teeth.

"Aren't you supposed to be surveilling or reconnoitering or whatever the hell it is you're supposed to be doing?"

"Nice, 'general,' can't remember which orders you gave to which soldiers? I've got time. Tobias isn't due for his nightly espresso run for a while."

"Isn't that the point, to see if he varies his routine?"

"I'm betting he won't. I wanted to talk to you. Alone. I get why you conscripted us for this little hit job; you really don't know anyone else. My ex, the one I didn't want to have to call, confirmed that Tobias and his goons didn't leave the house during the day. Neither did your brothers or their wives. Just a shift change with the van techs. So, either Tobias likes to tempt fate with his evening coffee breaks, or he needs the juice to get him through the night. I got this, Be ... Elizabeth. Don't sweat it."

"Why didn't you say anything back at Coit Tower?"

"I figured it was best to continue to let the others think you're in charge, no sense rocking the boat. Best *I* let you think you're in charge."

In two long strides, Sarah was in my face. It wasn't aggressive in a we're-going-to-fight kinda way, it was seductive; predatory, to be sure, but sensual.

"What are you doing?"

"I love you, Elizabeth, I have since that night."

"No, no, you don't. You're drawn to me, affected by me, because I made you, turned you. This isn't love, Sarah, this is ... this isn't right."

Undaunted, Sarah leaned in for a kiss. Her lips parted, her tongue darted forward. I clenched my teeth and pursed my lips. She tried to pry my mouth open with her tongue. I placed the palms on my hands on her shoulders and shoved, hard. Sarah sprang backward and landed on her back.

"Why, Elizabeth, why? Why do you turn me away?"

I stood up and assumed a fighting stance. My fists were balled, and my muscles were coiled, ready to strike.

"Just do your fucking job, Sarah. We have bigger issues here."

Sarah threw her arms down to her sides in a huff and uttered a primal scream that was neither human or animal.

She glared at me. Her mouth was agape, and her fangs glinted in the moonlight. She hissed.

And just like that, *poof,* Sarah transformed into a bat and flew off in the direction of Livermore and her objective. After a long moment, I sat back down on the rock I had been sitting on.

"What the fuck was that?" I had to say it out loud. I was incredulous. We had the weight of the world on our shoulders, the fate of our very existence was at stake, and Sarah wanted to start a love affair? Who the hell was I to talk, really? I was beginning to wonder if she was all-in, if maybe she might falter, or even worse, betray us. The crazy thing was, I still had no idea how I had turned Sarah into a vampire. It must have been me since she was so drawn to me, so attracted to me. There had to have been a co-mingling of fluids, but for the life of me, I did not remember at what point Sarah would have or could have drunk what qualified as my blood these days. I do remember a syrupy, metallic liquid on my lips when Andrei crucified me, but I don't recall how that got there either.

The bottom line was this, Sarah needed to carry out her assignment. My attraction to women was a new phenomenon. I didn't quite understand it other than the fact they had been women tainted by another vampire. We all go through the change differently, we all become something slightly different. And apparently, we are connected to our makers in some way. In my case, I am consumed with hatred for my mine. In Sarah's, she thought she was in love with hers.

I don't know why I hadn't given myself an assignment. That was elitist of me. I knew I would do my part when the time came, of that I had no doubt. But why I had left my comrades to do the reconnaissance and gather intelligence was beyond me. I knew what Sarah and Julie were going to do the rest of the night, but as for Andrei and Dietrich, although they'd pledged to do more tonight, I had no idea where they'd gone.

God, I was thirsty.

I transformed and flew off toward Alameda Point. There had been much hustle and bustle when I'd vectored over the old Navy base earlier in the evening. The area had been transformed in recent years. Real estate developers, unable to create meaningful affordable housing on the property, did manage to create a strip of restaurants and wine bars and turn it into a bit of a social gathering spot. Outdoor cafes, bar-and-grill-type joints with outdoor seating, pizza-by-the-slice shacks, a craft brewery, a skate park, and a gym lined a street across from abandoned aircraft hangars. A Christmas tree lot sat at the south end of Monarch Street.

Some of those outdoor seating areas offered a view of the water—the estuary to the north, the bay to the west. The estuary sliced Alameda from the mainland, made it an island, and fed San Leandro Bay, which in turn cut across what is known as Bay Farm Island. Island was a misnomer, as Bay Farm was connected to the mainland and bordered Oakland. Not many people were sitting outside, but plenty were out and about walking to and from establishments and their vehicles on the streets of the former air station. It gets chilly in Alameda in July, let alone early December. So I didn't expect that many folks eating outside.

What the hell was I going to do if there were? Turn West Red Line Avenue into my own personal buffet? It was too open here. The hunting ground was rich with game but there were too many witnesses and open spaces. It would be too conspicuous to drag someone off to one of the hangars, although it was fun to imagine leaving the remains in the middle of the tarmac for Alameda PD to find. I decided to continue on to Webster.

If Alameda had a bad neighborhood, it was Webster Street. With its beginning at Central Avenue and its end at the Webster Tube, the secondary drag was lined with local eateries of all ethnic varieties, bars—dingy dives and high-end cocktail lounges—chain restaurants—Taco Bell and McDonald's ... a pinball museum sat across the street from a sports collectibles shop.

Again, I doubted many pedestrians would be out this time of night, but there was a better chance that the ones who were would be ones who wouldn't be missed. Plus there were plenty of alleys and voids where I could drag a tasty morsel with which to have my way.

After the four-mile flight from the point to Webster, I found a cozy spot near a Pho place to become me again, and I started to stroll. I never did understand the fascination with Pho. It was like someone had dragged the bottom of a river, heated it up, and dumped it into a bowl.

Webster wasn't as crowded as I had hoped, but there were enough folks out and about, and there were certainly plenty of fast food connoisseurs if I really wanted to hit the drive-thru. That was a last resort, considering the last time I'd decided to dine on a lifetime of disappointment. I don't think I could ever forget the failed salesman who was unfortunate enough to pick me up at Taco Bell. There were enough burger joints to clog a few miles worth of arteries.

I found myself at the Fireside Lounge. They would be open for a few more hours. It was nestled between a taqueria and a sushi house. It was a red brick building with a neon sign trumpeting the name of the joint. Inside was warm and welcoming. This was the kind of place I would have frequented when I was alive. Great, long bar; dining tables and high-tops; inviting atmosphere.

The place featured a stage for live music acts, and I was relieved that there wasn't a band on this night. I wanted quiet. I wanted to stalk and hunt. A flyer on the wall showed the upcoming schedule, which included a drag show. Quite the spot.

The bar had every kind of alcohol you could imagine. I was thirsty, but it wasn't booze I craved. Young, virile, fit, handsome. That's was I needed. Male or female, it made no never mind. The bar was crowded but not full, and there were a few stools open. I took one at the end where I could survey the room and watch the comings and goings of the patrons. I ordered a Scotch I once again had no intention of drinking. I wasted more money this way. It wasn't my money anymore, but still.

Jukebox music blared as I stared at the honey-colored liquid and circled the top of the dram with my finger while the night wore on. It was starting to look like I was out of luck or that I was going to have to hit the drive-thru. And then *he* walked in.

He was tall, six-foot-four maybe? Broad shoulders, long legs, sexy five o'clock shadow expertly trimmed along the edges of his chiseled jaw, and high cheekbones. He wore form-fitting faded jeans with the cuffs rolled up, a black turtleneck sweater, a leather jacket, and dark brown dress boots. When he pulled his watch cap off his head, a trendy haircut was revealed—buzzed and faded on the sides, long and flowing on the top. He looked like a *Men's Fitness* magazine model.

He was pretty.

When he sauntered in, he seemed almost as lost as I had been. However, he had been to this place before, but he wasn't what you'd call a regular. The barmaid perked up as soon as she saw him. "What'll it be, handsome?"

"Vodka and cranberry … please."

"You got it, hun. Coming right up."

My elevator eyes took him in, every inch of him from head to toe, while he waited for his drink. I hovered over my own like I was some shy twenty-something that had never been in a bar before, while trying to look inconspicuous. The tall drink of water I had my eye on scanned the establishment with one boot on the hardwood and the other on the floor rail.

I willed him to glance in my direction. I mentally compelled him to look my way as I threw my furtive glance at him. He continued to check out the lounge looking at everything and everyone but me. Well, that shit didn't work.

When the barkeep finally brought him his drink, he was surprised. "You want to start a tab?"

"I'll pay as I go, thanks." He deftly handed her a folded bill with one hand and took his drink with the other. He was absentminded as he sipped through two swizzle straws. While the barmaid made change, this gorgeous hunk of soon-to-be blood donor finally turned his head my way.

He didn't look at me long enough for me to mesmerize him, but he knew I was there. An empty stool next to me beckoned. After one more scan of the room, he strolled to the end of the bar, and in a deep, melodic voice, asked, "Is this seat taken?"

"It is now."

"So, you don't mind if I join you?"

"Not at all."

In a previous … er … life, I would have fucked him right then and there. We've established that I am not a loose woman, but this was a guy I could really go for. Mid-to-late-thirties, light blue eyes, strapping, country strong, ruggedly handsome—but not in a manufactured or put on kinda way. He was fall-out-of-bed sexy.

There were a few cute guys at the spot, one or two that were a step above that, but this one … mmmmmmm. Yeah.

We made small talk. His name was Jack, he was from LA, went to USC but dropped out, wanted to be a writer, ended up a longshoreman instead. After working his way up the coast he ended up in Oakland working the docks. Jack had tried to get a few things published to no avail. He figured he could stretch his legs in the Bay Area, write something worth reading. I was reading him all right.

I spun him a tale about Pepperdine and public relations. I told him I was "in-between" jobs at the moment. I told him about Jessup, blah blah. How I was up for Public Relations Professional of the Year, blah blah blah. How my best friend was murdered by this serial killer. If I hadn't hooked him already, that did it.

I could have mesmerized him, but what fun would that be? This was different. I wanted to play. I laughed at his jokes, listened intently when he told me of his family, mom, dad, younger sister. Jack thought he was getting somewhere. Maybe he thought he was getting somewhere beyond a one-night stand. I wanted him to want me. I wanted him to desire me, lust for me, think maybe I was dating material.

Jack reminded me of the liberal rabble rouser I had dispatched in San Francisco. He had a similar look, a similar sensibility. But that guy was a target of opportunity, Jack was an antelope and I was a cheetah on the prowl.

He never did notice that I didn't take a sip from my glass while he downed three vodka and cranberries like they were tumblers of Kool-Aid. It was a bit odd that he didn't offer to buy me a drink. Cheap ass. He was a struggling writer turned longshoreman, after all. I wasn't going to hold it against him even though I wanted to.

Just then, a gaggle of half-drunk half-wits blew through the door. Two guys, three girls. They looked around and spotted my guy. He was six-four after all, hard to miss.

"Jack!"

The group jostled their way over to us and all of a sudden I felt small, like a fifth wheel. It was a fleeting feeling. It didn't take long to remember who I was. I knew I just needed to bide my time. It would be interesting to see if Jack was going to try to introduce me or include me or drag me along. This was not the first time I'd felt all alone in a room full of people. I really hoped he didn't try to introduce me. He wasn't the only prey animal in the neighborhood tonight. Jack looked delicious, but I wasn't going to put myself out there to get him. It had been a while since I had hunted for fun, for sport, but if this didn't work out, I'd survive.

Sometimes friends would meet up at one spot as a warm-up for the evening, have a drink or two, and then head out to the real happening for the night. I wondered if this was the warm-up or the destination. I figured I would find out soon enough.

I sat and pretended to sip my drink as I watched Jack

interact with his friends. He was quick to smile and even quicker to laugh. When he smiled his eyes smiled. He was the life of the party, the guy they wanted to hang out with, the guy they came to be with. Maybe it was his looks, maybe it was his writer's sensibilities. It all made me want him that much more.

Considering my perception of the collective IQ of the group when they'd arrived, I was pleased to learn my initial assessment was incorrect. Jack surrounded himself with a smart, witty clique.

And I couldn't wait to rob them of him.

"C'mon, Jack, time to go," a mousy brunette in a loose fitting knit cap implored. She had a button nose and a few scattered freckles on her cheeks.

"Yeah, Jack, let's hit it," a younger guy with sandy brown hair, glasses, and a face covered with moles said. He seemed to be the hanger-on. The rest of the crew started for the door.

"You know what, Maureen, I think I am going to stay here."

"You sure? We were going to head over to Telegraph in Oakland and hit a few bars over there. Isaiah and Tamara were going to show us a few new joints."

"Yeah, Jack, we're going to show the white folks how the other half really lives."

"Thanks for the offer, Isaiah, I'm going to make it an early night."

Isaiah clapped his hand on Jack's shoulder and looked him in the eye.

"Everything okay, Jack?"

"Yeah, you guys go on, have a good time. I'm fine."

"Tia might be there," Maureen chimed in.

"Well, you tell her I said 'hi' then."

"I'll do that."

With that, Jack's pals headed out into the East Bay night.

Jack let out a sigh and hung his head before heading back to the bar and ordering another drink. He took the glass as it was slid to him and staggered in my general direction. The alcohol was affecting him more than his machismo would admit, and he probably would have been worthless in the sack—whisky dick and all. Besides, I didn't want to make a habit of conventional intercourse. I liked my way better.

I wasn't about to burst his bubble. Had I been human, had I been an available single female, I would've played hard to get. I wouldn't have considered leaving the bar with him. Maybe I would've gotten his number. Probably. A date, a second date … several dates … then maybe, just maybe, I would've slept with him. He was too good looking and too sexy—maybe on the third date.

But I was not human.

I was not an available single woman on the prowl.

Well, that wasn't exactly true, now, was it?

I put on my best smolder and my green eyes locked on to his now bloodshot orbs.

"Whaddaya say, sailor? How about we blow this popsicle stand?"

"I was just going to ask you the same thing, only not so colloquially."

"Well, I'm a little old school. I like you, Jack. You're pretty."

"I don't think anyone has ever called me that, and I am in no condition to argue. I didn't catch your name."

"I didn't throw it."

We exited the bar and found ourselves in the chilly Alameda night air. We walked along Webster toward Oakland. He offered his arm; I took it. The garlic odor wafting from the opposing pizza joints on opposite sides of the street was almost unbearable. I grabbed Jack's arm tighter. My discomfort with one of the instruments of my potential destruction helped with my romantic ruse. He grabbed my hand with his free one and pulled me closer.

We crossed Santa Clara and Haight, and then crossed Webster at Lincoln. Jack led me to the back of a small corner market. Stone stairs led to a weathered door with a round, brass knob. A big, obnoxious security light mounted on what looked like a thirty-foot tall flagpole blinded me. I pulled my arm away and shielded my eyes.

"Yeah, that takes some getting used to."

Like there would be any getting used to anything in this scenario. We climbed the steps as Jack fished out the key. He inserted it into the doorknob, turned it in one smooth motion, and pushed it open with a well-placed shoulder.

"Forgive the mess."

I felt like a romantic comedy cliché as I slow-walked the Spartan excuse of an apartment. A table lamp with a low wattage bulb was the only illumination, a stark contrast after the four bajillion candlepower security light outside. A small four-burner electric stove sat in the corner of the kitchenette. A dinette sat in the middle of that space. A low-slung coffee table and a well-worn futon occupied what was supposed to be the living room. The only thing in the flat that didn't scream starving artist was the enormous LCD television that sat atop a makeshift entertainment center. He seemed to notice me noticing.

"I like football, and I like watching it on the big screen. Make yourself at home."

Now, had I not just emerged from a cistern in a void in an eighty-year-old island prison, I might have been in a position to bitch about the Gorton's Fisherman's digs. But considering the places I had called home, I wasn't about to criticize my host. If he offered to make Ramen noodles, I would have to progress the evening.

"Can I get you something? Water? Soda? Something stronger, perhaps?"

Had I been that available single woman I would have taken him up on his hospitality.

"I'm thirsty all right."

Jack hung his coat on a hook on the back of the entry door and turned toward the inner space of the apartment.

He found me in his face, in his space, as he completed that turn.

"Um ..."

He didn't get a chance to form a word. I kissed him full on the mouth. My tongue parted his lips and his teeth and searched for his. I pawed at him, as a soft, playful growl reverberated in my throat. He put his hands on my shoulders and pushed me back, breaking the kiss.

"Whoa, slow down there."

"Don't you want me, Jack? Hmmmm?"

I was teasing him, taunting him as I undressed in front of him. Slowly. Sensually. His jaw dropped as he took me in. That night with Jonas had awakened something in me that was dormant, dead even. I felt a warmth ... a heat ... from my loins I hadn't felt since I was, well, alive. I had all but given up on traditional sex because of my transformation. But now, well, I was horny as hell.

"Um. Yeah." He swallowed hard. "Of course, I'm just not used to ..."

"What Jack? What aren't you used to?"

"Give me a second here."

His brawny side came out as he pushed the coffee table out of the way and flung the futon open to the sleeping, or fucking, position. Jack kicked off his boots and unbuttoned his jeans. He struggled with the denim as his impatience and lust surfaced. One leg was still caught when I rushed him and pulled his sweater over his head.

I think that one foot was still in the pant leg when I pushed him back on the futon and mounted him. Since my vagina didn't generate lubrication anymore, initial penetration was uncomfortable. His hips rose to meet my grinding. After several long moments, he tried to flip me to missionary position. I drove my palms into his pectoral muscles and pushed him back onto his shoulder blades. He tried to reach for my breasts. I pushed him back down again. If I hadn't had other plans, I might have let him touch me. I might have even taken him in my mouth. But this wasn't that kind of party.

I continued to ride him until I felt a swelling, an increase in hardness, and I knew he was getting ready to climax. My head tipped back, and my razor sharp canines extended. I grabbed his hair just above his forehead and turned his head to the side and sank my fangs into the jugular vein in his neck. The dark red liquid flowed fast into my hungry mouth as he emptied himself into me. I sucked slowly and deliberately, enjoying every ounce, every drop. I lapped up any stream of blood that tried to get away. I shuddered and quivered with my own orgasm. It rose from my loins and came in waves. I opened and closed my thighs as if Jack were a thigh master. I took my time. I savored Jack—his blood and his member. It never did go soft.

Jack's eyes glassed over. His breathing slowed and then stopped. His heartbeat slowed and then stopped. Jack was gone. And I had enjoyed every second of him. Rarely do you find someone pretty *and* smart. There's an exception to every rule, I suppose.

My dismount was as graceful as it could be. I really didn't care for the spunk running down the inside of my leg. Condoms were always a must when I had been human. Sex was always a messy, sloppy act, and since I wasn't ready to have kids back then, guys didn't get to do their business inside me. Didn't really matter now, did it?

For once I was smart enough to feed in the nude. I didn't have to worry about bloodstained clothes and wandering around all conspicuous. Not that it was going to be a problem tonight. I padded my way over to the sink in the kitchenette and cleaned up the best I could, including my vagina and inner thighs. I got dressed appreciably faster than I had disrobed.

I opened the door and stepped into the God-awful light of that fucking security lamp. Just as I started to shimmy up a drain pipe to the roof, Jack's pals from the bar came barreling into the parking lot. They called out to me. I heard them talk among themselves.

"Hey, you!"

"Holy shit, did you see that?"

"Isn't that the chick from the bar?"

They clambered up the steps. Fuck, I forgot to lock the door. The drain pipe broke loose as they tried to follow me. As I prepared to transform, I could hear their horror as they found their dead friend on the futon.

The most athletic of the bunch scrambled to the rooftop and tried to hoist himself up. He was only visible from the chest up as I sprinted into bat form and flew off.

If I didn't have bad luck I wouldn't have any, I swear. I'd had it all planned out. Well, almost. The plan didn't coalesce until I got to Webster. The plan was aborted on Alameda Point because of the openness of the area. But a target of opportunity, denser architecture, and serendipity had made this the perfect kill. That is, until the club goers, the bar hoppers, decided to end the night with their pal Jack.

As my flight path took me on a vector out of Alameda, police sirens pierced the silence of that otherwise quiet community.

CHAPTER XVIII

The flight back to Coit Tower was agonizing. I was hypersensitive, having just fed and having my escape interrupted. My head was on a swivel as every headlight, every streetlight, the search and fuselage lights of a police helicopter, the beacons on top of the Bay Bridge, all made my flying erratic. My wings dipped, and I damn near went into a barrel roll before I righted myself and managed to block out the distractions. Well, except for a seagull that'll never be the same after a near midair collision.

I was the first of my merry little band to made it back to Coit Tower. I was glad for that. The cold, hard cement was welcoming as I found a place to sit and reflect. In another life, I could have loved Jack. Love is the wrong word. I would have enjoyed Jack. Dammit. I had enjoyed him. Ugh.

You know what I mean. I could've dated him. He was handsome and sexy and intelligent and oh so many things I liked in a guy. But those days are long gone, and I wanted to have some fun. I wanted to enjoy the hunt. Using my abilities as a seductress was empowering and intoxicating.

Feeding out of necessity was, well, necessary. But this, this was different, and I didn't do this often enough. I just could have done without the fucking interruption. I was just glad I had finished and was on my way out. I could only imagine what would have happened if Jack's cadre of friends had walked in on me draining their buddy dry. Jack wouldn't have been the only dead body in that tiny apartment. I knew damn well nobody was going to believe the guy who saw me flap off into the night.

Damn. That thought was actually delicious in hindsight. An orgy of blood. By choice. Not because I hadn't fed in two nights, but because I wanted it. The thought was thrilling, electric. Missed opportunity. I made a mental note. Maybe I'd go back to Alameda and hang out with Jack's pals and party with them, Elizabeth style.

Dietrich was next with Andrei close behind. The girls were lagging, and I hoped it was because they were going to have good information to share. I had a feeling it was going to be awkward with Sarah. She was going to have to be dealt with after we took care of the Order of the Mazda RX-7.

"Elizabeth."

"Andrei."

"You look like a vampire who has recently fed."

"Well, that's none of your fucking business, now, is it?"

"Easy, progeny."

"Don't, don't you dare."

"Hey, you two, aren't we supposed to be working together? Weren't you guys walking arm in arm just a few nights ago?"

There was no way in hell I was going to apologize to the prick, but Jonas was right. I shouldn't have snapped at Andrei, but I wasn't in the mood for his shit either.

Julie was the next to arrive.

"Where's Sarah?"

"Dunno, haven't seen her."

"What do you mean you haven't seen her?"

"Exactly what I just said, Liz, I haven't seen her all night."

"I hope she did her fucking job."

"You saw her though, didn't you, Elizabeth?"

"How the fuck do you know that, Andrei?"

"That's none of your fucking business."

"Oh, now who's using foul language? Breaking your own rule, aren't you?"

"If the situation calls for it …"

"Jesus Christ, is that what you guys are going to do all night, argue?"

Sarah arrived in the middle of the donnybrook.

"Where the fuck have you been?"

"None of your goddamn business. And what about you,

Elizabeth, what have you been doing? Especially while the rest of us were out doing your dirty work."

"Jesus Christ, is everyone going to be up in my shit tonight?"

"That's not what I smell." Dietrich's nose was sniffing the air like a dog who caught a good whiff. He grew despondent as he realized what it was. Andrei just started cackling and wandered off to a void in the wall. Julie and Sarah taunted me as if we were schoolgirls.

"Who was he, Liz?"

"Yeah, Elizabeth, tell us all about him. Was he good in the sack? Did he have a big di ..."

"Who I feed on and who I fuck is none of your concern. Do you two want to go? I am flush with blood, and I am wound tight. Do you bitches really think you can take me?"

"Sorry, Liz, I didn't mean ..."

"Let's get to it, shall we?"

Andrei drifted back to our group.

I was still wondering how the hell I got put in charge of this little hit squad. Military was not my thing; I had never served. Sure, I took charge in meetings, but never anything like this. Here I was organizing and directing recon missions and plotting an assault and an assassination.

"Ahura Mazda is not what they once were," Andrei volunteered. "Tobias is their leader. There are a few cells here and there around the globe, Prague, Istanbul, Hong Kong, Rio, squad leaders, but what we are dealing with is the main strike force, the elite."

I looked at him incredulously. "How the hell …?"

"Don't ask questions you don't want answers to."

"Okay, then. Julie?"

"Well, there are a few less surveillance techs to deal with. Let's just say they're wintering along the way to Half Moon Bay. Everyone else is still holed up at your parents' house. It looks like they think you're stupid enough to go back there."

"Dietrich?"

Jonas just stared at the ground.

"Jonas!"

"Um, yeah, so, I don't think a full frontal assault on the house is a good idea. If they are what everyone thinks and says they are, there will be booby traps. It figures that they'll have some way to detect us since we don't show up on camera. Our body temps are lower than humans so they'll have equipment for that."

"What about SFPD or any other John Q. Laws?"

"Well, Ahura Mazda must have some kind of influence, because Tim's death is not even a consideration, which is unusual because cops are usually out for blood after one of their own is murdered, and with the wife on top of that … so nothing, no chatter. Not hearing anything about FBI or ATF either."

"Sarah?"

"What?"

"Keep up the attitude, so help me …"

"Keep your panties on. Oh, wait."

Andrei stepped between me and Sarah before I could

bitch slap her fangs right out of her head. "What an interesting web you weave, Elizabeth. Interesting indeed." I had bigger problems than two jilted lovers. What a demented love triangle this was turning out to be. The funny thing was, I'd killed the one I was really attracted to.

"Okay, okay. Tobias did the same thing, at the same exact time. No deviation."

That settled it.

I would have liked a bigger sample size of data than just two nights, but God only knew how long these vampire hunters would stay at my folks' house using my brothers and their wives as bait.

"Tomorrow night, we take Tobias. If we cut off the head, Ahura Mazda will fall."

"What are you going to do, fuck him to death?"

"Bitch! I have had about all I am going to take from you tonight."

I flew to Sarah and grabbed her by the throat. One long, sharp fingernail extended from my right index finger and threatened to pierce the soft flesh under her chin. "One more word, and I will end you."

She landed with a hard 'thud' as I tossed her aside. I was pretty sure she'd gotten the message, or at least the look in her eyes said as much.

"It's getting late; we should all get to our sanctuaries. Let's all meet in Livermore tonight. You guys take out the heavies and the techs. I'll handle Tobias."

"Why do you …"

In a soft yet stern voice, I said, "Sarah … what did I tell you?"

What a petulant child. Thank God I didn't find her attractive that way. She would have driven me nuts as a girlfriend. In any case, I was sick and tired of her whining and her advances. She would have to be dealt with when this was over.

"Jonas, before you come, make sure you check the police band and see if we've popped up on the radar."

"Yeah, you got it."

"Andrei, I'll assume you'll just do Andrei things?"

"Whatever that means, *Szerelem*."

"Oooookay, then. Julie, see you there?"

"Yep, I'll be there with bells on."

Ever the perky one.

"Max Baer Park, nine o'clock, sharp."

"Sir, yes, sir!"

Before I could sock her one, Sarah transformed and flew off. Julie bounced for the elevators, and Andrei vanished into the fog. I was left with Jonas.

"Really, did you have to sleep with him? I can still smell him on you."

"Well, there wasn't any sleeping."

"You know what I mean. Alameda PD is besides themselves. Murders don't happen there very often. They want your head on a pike, or whoever's responsible. This character you … well, you know, was pretty well regarded."

"I can see why. He was yummy."

"That's not the point, is it, Elizabeth?"

"No, Jonas. What exactly is your point? We have a little coffin romp and all of a sudden we're dating? All of a sudden we're exclusive? Give me a break."

It sickened me to say hurtful things to my dear, sweet detective. I didn't mean to wound him. But my seduction of Jack certainly had done that. On one hand, I didn't care. I'd enjoyed it. On the other hand, Jonas and I did find comfort in each other's arms. And I wasn't sure what that meant. That was something else I was going to have to deal with once Ahura Mazda was eliminated.

"Look, this isn't the time or the place to have this conversation. We've got other things to worry about. Let's pick this up when we don't have a squad of vampire hunting storm troopers all over our ass."

"Yeah, guess so. You're right. I just thought …"

I sashayed over to him and kissed Jonas softly on the lips. After I broke the kiss I replaced my lips with an index finger. "Shhhhh. Soon." I just hoped we'd get that chance.

CHAPTER XIX

I awoke that night refreshed. Less than twenty-four hours after being freshly fed and fucked, I was surprised I wasn't thirsty. My condition never ceased to amaze. I wondered if I would ever learn to control it or stave it off like Andrei could. And what of Dietrich? How did he subsist? Did he rely on connections at the local blood banks? Obviously, he had let it get the better of him when he dispatched my poor Whitney. As for Tweedledee and Tweedledum, I didn't give a fuck what they fed on as long as they left babies and kids alone.

Getting ready this night was a slow, deliberate affair. I picked out a pair of patent-leather, thigh-high boots, a black miniskirt, a tight black sweater, and a black three-quarter-length trench coat. Tactical. You may wonder, "Why, Elizabeth, where did you get such things?" Never you mind.

I got dressed, did my best to avoid the park rangers, and headed for a secluded spot on Alcatraz Island. Before long, I was airborne and headed for Livermore. No stopovers this time. Straight to Max Baer Park. Hopefully, my compatriots were up to the task on this night. Eventually Tobias and the Order of Ahura Mazda would move on and formulate another plan. That night with bumblebee bat had been serendipity, as it gave me, I mean us, the upper hand.

We all arrived within minutes of each other this time. There was no waiting. The girls gave me side eye, Andrei barely acknowledged me, and Dietrich, well, let's just say he needed to roll his tongue back up into his mouth. Guess it was the outfit.

"Okay, here's the plan. After Tobias heads out for his nightly constitutional, girls, take out the support staff and the outdoor guards. Andrei—everyone on the inside. My brothers and their wives are off limits. You got it?"

He nodded without hesitation.

"What are you going to do?" Julie asked.

"Dietrich and I will handle Tobias."

Sarah rolled her eyes and cast her gaze in the direction of my parents' house.

"What are we to do in the meantime? It's going to be a while before Tobias goes out for coffee."

"Take up positions near the house and be ready. That way you can see if any routines change or if they bring in more personnel. Give us time to get to the cafe before you do what you're going to do."

"Whatever you say."

We all fanned out and headed toward my folks' house on Fluorite Court. Sarah and Julie climbed trees near the surveillance vans, and Dietrich hung back with me across the street. Andrei, well, he must've gone off to do Andrei things. He had developed this annoying habit of just vanishing. He had been invaluable in gathering intel for this lightning strike commando raid, so I had little doubt that he would do his job. It was the girls I was worried about, especially Sarah. But self-preservation seemed to be important to both of them.

This operation was going to be the most important thing I had ever done. This was survival. Failure meant death and destruction, even though I didn't think we were all going to make it through this night. And that was fine. I was worried about Julie, considering I had gotten her into this mess. I would prefer she stuck around, but Andrei and Sarah, I couldn't care less. Jonas, on the other hand, I had grown quite fond of, despite his petty jealousy.

The wait was interminable. We couldn't do anything until Tobias left. There was no way we could cut the head off the snake if the whole platoon was hunkered down in my parents' house. It would be a shooting gallery. Now, regular bullets just seemed to make holes and didn't have a lethal effect, but I had to think these fools had to have weapons and ammunition that could take us down. I don't know if they wanted to risk close, hand-to-hand combat considering our strength advantage, but I wasn't willing to take that risk.

Julie and Sarah were getting itchy in their respective trees. They had plenty of foliage for cover. The rustling, on the other hand, was threatening to give them away. I didn't dare shush them. I thought I saw a six-foot tall puff of smoke or mist on the roof near the chimney. It was gone as fast as it appeared. A smile curled my lips. I knew what it was.

At the appointed time, Tobias emerged from the house and was accompanied by two large, muscled bodyguards. He paused for a moment to give the door guards instructions and then headed off to the cafe at a brisk pace. Jonas and I followed at a safe distance. We slowed as I summoned a few bats to keep eyes, and ears, on things while we handled our end.

Within minutes, I heard a quartet of free-tailed bats vector toward the house behind us. I was always amazed at how quickly they heeded my call.

"Don't trust the girls?" Jonas whispered.

"No." And we left it at that.

We ducked behind trees and telephone poles when we needed to. Every so often, Tobias's escorts stopped and surveyed the area. We could have taken them out during the walk, but I didn't want to raise an alarm with the rest of Ahura Mazda or the local police. The plan was to slip into a booth with Tobias while Jonas handled the goons and emptied the cafe. Then I would take Tobias apart.

That was the plan anyway.

I split from Jonas and wound my way to the back of the cafe. Slipping through the service entrance, I waited for my quarry to arrive. Within minutes, the bell over the door jingled. I couldn't see what was going on in the coffee shop, but my combat air patrol was showing me what was happening back at the house. My head twitched and I shivered as I watched Sarah and Julie rip the techs from the vans and tear into them in the middle of the street. I didn't think they had it in them to be honest. I thought they would choke when push came to shove. When I happened upon them they were resorting to feeding on youngsters and now ... well, shit, survival was one helluva motivator.

Another bat was outside a picture window that gave her an unobstructed view of the inside of the house. A fog spilled out from the fireplace into the main living space and the dining area. Looks of confusion were exchanged between my brothers and my sisters-in-law as the Ahura Mazda soldiers readied their weapons and took up positions.

Andrei never made himself visible, and he killed them all.

Blood splashed across the window, obscuring my bat's view. But she could still hear. Gunfire. Screaming. Anguish. Paolo went crashing through the big picture window onto the front lawn. His wife rushed to his aid, but she was grabbed and thrown backward by a tentacle of gray fog. Laser sights and tracer bullets penetrated Andrei's mist, but they didn't penetrate him. Stavros was picked up by an unseen force and broken in half in midair.

That gray cloud enveloped the downstairs of the house.

The outdoor guards ran toward the street when they heard Julie and Sarah tearing the techs to pieces. Julie never saw the bullets coming. The first three hit her square in the back. She arched as she fell, and the fourth round pierced her skull. It exited through her right eye. She wasn't coming back this time.

It took every ounce of self-control I could muster not to scream as I watched my best friend die … again. But I had to stick to the plan. I knew there might be casualties, but I honestly hadn't thought … oh, God … Julie. I had to break the mental connection to the bats; I couldn't take any more. The last thing I saw was one of the Order of Ahura Mazda blast several rounds into Stavros's wife.

I burst through the kitchen door into the seating area and found Tobias sipping his espresso. I was seething. The plan to sit with Tobias and interrogate him was abandoned. What I didn't quite understand was the silence in and around the place. Where the fuck was Jonas? Where the fuck was the staff?

Tobias didn't say a word. He just sipped his coffee with a smug grin on his face.

Jonas was supposed to handle the escort and clear the cafe. Flanked by Tobias's guards, he stepped into view from behind the counter. He had a baseball bat in his hands. "Sorry, Elizabeth." He swung the bat at my head.

The last thing I saw was Dietrich's dusty brown Oxfords and the bottom of his trench coat. *Motherfu* …

CHAPTER XX

When I came to I was upright, strapped to a flat wooden platform reminiscent of the night of my abduction. There were some key differences, however. This time I was clothed, I wasn't bleeding as far I could tell, and there wasn't a smarmy Eurotrash vampire circling me. I was in a fog, I had no idea where I was, and my vision was blurry. And I had a splitting headache.

What I didn't quite understand was why I couldn't break my bonds. I should have been able to snap these ropes like string, but there was a burning sensation in the skin of my wrists as I struggled. Thankfully, my boots kept the bindings from making contact with the skin of my ankles. Regardless, my supernatural, or preternatural if you prefer, strength was useless.

As my vision cleared and my surroundings came into focus I saw Tobias. He was sitting cross-legged in a simple wooden chair. He was perfectly still and dressed impeccably. When I'd seen him at the cafe I hadn't had much time to take him in before Dietrich had cleaned my clock. He reminded me of Andrei in some ways. He was also the polar opposite in others. Tobias was well-appointed and debonair. Immaculately groomed. Not a hair out of place, clean-shaven. He was staring at me.

We were in a large metal enclosure of some kind. It was just me and him. It seemed too large to be a shipping container. It was a perfect rectangle, so that ruled out storage shed or manufactured house. The walls appeared to be sturdy and thick, the floor was a cement slab, and the roof or ceiling, or whatever it was, was flat.

"You'd make a terrible Bond villain, you know that?" I spat at Tobias.

He responded with a sly grin and a playful huff. Tobias then pulled out a pack of Gitanes and a Zippo lighter. Thick aromatic smoke hung in the air after he lit the cigarette and took the first drag. The act of lighting the cigarette was more demonstration than nicotine need. He wanted to show me that our environment was airtight.

"You got one of those for me, you prick?"

Tobias stood and regarded me as he smoked his Gitane. He was quiet and deliberate. Smooth. No wasted movement.

"You truly are remarkable. I don't think I have ever come across one such as you."

His words disarmed me. There was a respect, awe even. It wasn't so much his word choice as it was the inflection. He was confident. He was not scared in the least. But Tobias respected me. Unlike Andrei, with whom I could use sarcasm and bullying to get under his skin, I didn't have a strategy or a play here.

"Your shape-shifting abilities alone have become ... legendary. And I don't think you are quite finished ... evolving."

"I feel plenty evolved. Let me loose, and I'll show you just how evolved."

Really, Elizabeth? This is the witty banter you come up with?

"I'm sure you'd like that, wouldn't you?"

"What is it with you people? The monologuing, the grandstanding, the theatrics? You guys all flunk out of Julliard? Untie me, and I'll pop a straw in you and drain you like a juice box."

Tobias huffed again as he took one last drag from his cigarette, threw it to the floor, and crushed it out with his foot.

"Your tongue isn't going to get you out of this, Elizabeth. When I finish with you, I'll make sure Andrei and Sarah meet similar fates."

"What about Julie?"

"Ah, yes, poor Miss Engstrom. Well, as luck would have

it, a bullet to the brain pan is quite enough to dispatch one of your kind." He pointed to the base of his skull.

As Tobias finished his sentence, hissing the word "kind," I thought I saw the flash of an animal eye shine in the corner of the container.

"Then why don't you do me like that? Bullet to the brain. Simple, easy."

Tobias ignored my taunts.

"Your bindings have been soaked in garlic brine and coated in garlic salt. If you cast your gaze upward, you'll see a rather large cross. It is modeled after the Heroes' Cross in the Carpathian Mountains. This ... this ..." Tobias indicated the confines that we found ourselves within. "Mouse-trap, if you will. This box is perfectly constructed to dispose of you."

So, there it was. There was no negotiating, no insulting my way to freedom, no bullying my way out of this.

"Okay, I was wrong. That is what you are, a cheesy, smarmy Bond villain. You make Blofeld look like a genius."

"How very droll. Your popular cultural insults do not faze me. Ah, Ian, he was a great writer and a wonderful friend. Unfortunately, he died way too young."

Obviously, I had underestimated my opponent, and I had a sinking feeling that Andrei's intel had been lacking. Something told me Ahura Mazda was not a weak shell of its former self, but alive and well and on the hunt for vampires. I scanned the container for any possible exits. I looked for surveillance cameras as well. I might not show up on video, but Tobias sure as hell did. Perhaps his security detail was keeping a close eye on what was going on. They'd be able to tell if he was getting thrashed about. I couldn't imagine that they would leave their leader alone with a supernatural, shape-shifting predator. But that's what it looked like. Tobias figured the garlic ropes and the ceiling-mounted cross would be enough to keep him safe. It smelled like a fucking Olive Garden in here.

I did feel weak and tired. Defeat was overtaking me. I was starting to resign myself to my fate. I'd known Julie was dead, but Tobias's confirmation punched me in the face. I had survived Andrei and the transformation, I had survived Da Rocha and I don't know how many fucking cops. I had almost drowned. I had been trapped in an abandoned coal mine. Dietrich. Fucker.

Tobias reached inside his suit jacket. I thought he was going to pull out another cigarette. I was mistaken. He pulled out a long cylindrical wooden stake sharpened to a point. I gasped when I saw it. Tobias walked to a dark corner of the container and picked up a large hammer.

So, this was it. This is how I go. This is the story of me. I know I had thought that before, but this time I could not envision a way out of this.

Was that eye shine?

The other effect the garlic-soaked ropes had on me was disconcerting. I couldn't transform. Usually, my fight-or-flight response would kick in, and I would become something and make my escape. But Tobias's talismans were working in that regard. Now he was bearing down on me with a wooden stake and a hammer. The stake was no doubt intended for my heart.

"I take no pleasure in this, Elizabeth. You are unnatural, you are the spawn of an evil being, and you and your kind must be stamped out."

"Wait, wait, wait, no, I could help you, yeah, I could help you hunt down other vampires, I could be like a vampire mercenary, yeah …"

Tobias hesitated. But only for a moment.

He walked to my left, and his right hand unlocked the hinge for the table I was lashed to. It, and I, swung into a horizontal position. It locked into position with a "thunk." Tobias moved alongside, the stake in his right hand, the hammer in his left.

"A southpaw, eh? So, no incantations? No rituals? No priest?"

"I am fully ordained, *vampire*. No need for ceremony. I have all that I need." He actually spat on the floor after the word "vampire."

Tobias placed the point of the stake above my heart, the tip touching and piercing my flesh. It must have been blessed because it burned. He raised the hammer high above his head as I squirmed and cursed underneath him.

"Let me go, Tobias."

He tapped his ear with the hammer. I could just make out some kind of earplug or in-ear listening device, an earbud of some kind. My voice had no effect.

There was an agonizing pause as I waited for the strike and waited to be ended.

Blackfoot, growling and mewling with claws fully extended, flew out of a darkened corner and struck Tobias in the face. She scratched and bit and hissed while Tobias flailed with the hammer and stake. Blackfoot tore at his face. Blood flew and splashed and spurted. Some splattered across my face. Tobias dropped his weapons and tried to pry my cat off his shredded and bloody face. He grabbed her by the scruff of her neck and pulled her off.

*"**Put her down, Tobias.**"* For a split second, my hypnotic voice had him. I was afraid he was going to hurl Blackfoot against the wall and hurt her or worse. Blackfoot calmed when she heard my command and Tobias set her down on the concrete. He shook his head, tapped the earbuds, cleared the cobwebs, and started looking around for the hammer and stake. His face looked like he had tried to shave with a cheese grater. I was pretty sure he couldn't see. Either his eyes had been gouged out or they were clouded with torn skin and blood.

The smell of Tobias's free-flowing blood had me in a frenzy. I struggled against the ropes, but I could not break free. I thought maybe Blackfoot would chew through the ropes, but this wasn't a movie, and she was already in the corner cleaning herself. She had this "my work is done here" air about her.

Tobias was swinging the hammer wildly. I wasn't too concerned about him hitting pay dirt with that thing, but even a blind squirrel finds a nut. My ears were assaulted with a horrific cacophony of banging metal. I heard voices, but I couldn't make them out. The one door to the container, one that had been hidden from view, flew open.

Andrei.

"You have got to be fucking kidding me."

In his signature ensemble, Andrei stepped through the opening. He found Tobias stabbing at the air. My maker tackled our would-be assassin and made short work of him, snapping his neck with a bone-crunching twist.

"You try my patience, progeny."

"Don't ever call me that again."

"You do want to be liberated, yes? You do want to be untied, yes? Save your indignation for another time. For now, we go."

Andrei produced a knife from his inside jacket pocket and cut through the ropes that had kept me at bay. He pulled his pocket square and wiped the garlic juice from my ankles and wrists.

"Come, Elizabeth, car waiting."

When we exited the container that was to have been my permanent coffin, we found Sarah in the middle of a ring of dead Ahura Mazda soldiers. They were in various stages of mutilation. Sarah was covered with blood and mercenaries. "Hi, baby, mwah."

"What the fuck?"

"No time, car, go now. Sarah, let's move."

The strain of sirens kicked up in the distance and echoed off the nearby buildings. We were at the docks in Oakland. Tobias had meant to bury me at sea in a watery grave. So, the stake to the heart wasn't enough. Drowning me and leaving me at the bottom of the harbor were to be thrown in for good measure ... as was I, apparently.

Just as we climbed into a black BMW sedan, I looked back and saw Blackfoot exit the metal box and pad off into the night, careful to avoid the dead paramilitary guys strewn about. Sarah hit the push start as Andrei and I hopped in the back seat and closed the doors. Sarah's face glistened with blood that dripped down and covered her chin, neck, and chest to her décolletage. I must admit, I thought she was hot at that moment.

"Go, go, go!"

Andrei was insistent. I had never seen him flustered or panicked. But I had always gotten the impression that he didn't care for the attention of John Q. Law either. Before long, Sarah had pointed the car south along I-880. No one talked. Well, I counted street lamps under my breath, but there was no actual conversation.

We exited onto 92 and headed for the San Mateo Bridge. I had a feeling I knew where we were going. I wasn't sure how Sarah could have managed to hang on to her house in her current state, but since she had been hanging out with Andrei, nothing was out of the realm of possibility. I hadn't been back there since the night I fucked her and killed her. Her car was at the bottom of the Bay. And beyond plotting our commando raid that had gone horribly wrong, I really had no idea what any of these fuckers had been up to.

Sarah's house was dark when we pulled into the driveway. We exited the car. Sarah punched in a code in the keypad affixed to the garage door frame, and the automatic opener did its job. The smell of old motor oil and gasoline hit me in the face as we walked in.

The gregarious, bitter, bi-curious former real estate agent started flipping light switches as we entered the kitchen. This was the first time I had noticed that Andrei was barefoot. This reminded me of the night at Sutro Baths when he had crucified Julie and tussled with me and Jonas.

Jonas. I could barely think his name without seething.

"We all need to get cleaned up. Who wants to shower first? Sarah, did you bring ..."

"Yes, Andrei, I brought your clothes. Elizabeth and I could, you know, um, shower together, isn't that right, Beth?"

"Nobody. Calls. Me. Beth. And if I recall, the last time we did that, it didn't go so well for you."

"Fuck you."

"Ladies, enough. I will shower, then Elizabeth, and then you, Sarah. We are your guests, after all."

Andrei left us to talk or make out or fight or whatever. He made his way to the bathroom and started the water. Sarah and I just stood at opposite ends of the kitchen staring at each other.

"What the fuck happened, Liz?"

"Detective Sergeant Jonas Dietrich happened. He cold-cocked me with a baseball bat as I was about to tune Tobias up. Next thing you know, Tobias is introducing me to the pointy end. How the hell did you guys find me?"

"Andrei. He got one of the Mazda guys to talk. I don't know how, and I don't think you want to know either. The guy was crying and asking for his mother by the time Andrei was done within him. I think he was thankful when I snapped his neck." Sarah was absentmindedly wiping her face and neck with a kitchen towel while she explained interrogation techniques that would have made the Gestapo blush.

"Well, I'll say this once, and that'll be the end of it, I don't want to make a thing out of it. Thank you."

"Don't thank me. I wanted to leave you there to rot. It was Andrei's idea."

"Thanks all the same."

"Welcome."

"We need to talk."

"No, we don't."

"Um, yeah, we do. I have some questions for you, missy, and you're going to fucking answer them."

"Not until I've had a shower. Care to join me? Oh, wait,

yeah, that's how we got in this fucking mess in the first place."

"Bitch."

"Now, now. You're in my house. You're not going to fuck me and steal my clothes this time."

Andrei emerged from the master suite in a fresh black suit and white dress shirt. Shoes covered his disgusting animal feet.

"Do you ever wear anything else?"

He looked down at himself and held his arms out wide.

"What? What's wrong with what I wear?"

"Never mind."

"Who is next, ladies?"

Sarah didn't answer; she just pounded off for the master bedroom and the shower. So much for showering in order. I guess it didn't really matter.

"Did I miss something, Elizabeth?"

"No, she's just jealous, angry, and bitter. She thinks she's in love with me. She can't forgive me for turning her and abandoning her."

"My dear, you cannot blame yourself for her wants and desires. When we become we bring something of our past selves with us, but we are also something new."

"I don't even know how I made her."

"In your throes of passion, she drank of your blood. It is the only way. After she died a mortal death, she arose as one of the undead."

"But I don't remember ... and I sure as fuck don't

remember how your blood got into my mouth either, if we're going with your logic here."

Andrei put his finger to his lips as if to shush me, but I had more questions. How could I not remember Sarah biting me, or did I make it so she could drink from me? Goddammit. Had I really been that so far gone into that shower session that I'd lost myself utterly?

"Fuck you, Andrei, seriously, nobody shushes me. Tell me this, why didn't you kill Sarah? I was attracted to her because you tainted her in the first place. Why didn't you kill her? I seem to kill all those I feed on."

"I would like to tell you that it's self-control. But, alas, it's not as narcissistic as all that, I'm afraid. I had seduced our friend, and she brought me back here. I broke with my, how you say, *modus operandi*, and decided I would have her without my usual … ambience. Her boyfriend had a key. I was interrupted."

"So, you didn't want to fight the guy?"

"I abhor violence."

"Oh, that's rich. But you didn't have a problem dispatching Da Rocha."

"That was survival."

"What about Christina, Dietrich's girlfriend, or whatever, why was she still walking around?"

"You'll have to ask our dear detective."

"I intend to."

"You should go to her."

Andrei tilted his head, and I looked toward the master suite. I couldn't believe what Andrei was suggesting.

"Look, fucker, I may have made her, but I am not into her."

"Go, Elizabeth. She needs you."

"I never needed you."

I couldn't believe I was actually going. The carpet was soft and plush, and my boots sank into it as I made my way to Sarah's bedroom, the master suite. She was at her makeup table, dressed in a big, puffy white robe, and she was brushing her wet hair. I was silent as I approached. I thought it was odd that she was sitting in front of a mirror although she cast no reflection in the glass. Maybe it was the familiarity, the comfort of the act. I placed my hands on her shoulders. Sarah paused for a moment before laying her head on the back on my hand.

"Why do you hate me?"

"Oh, honey, I don't hate you. I just don't know what to do with you. I don't know you. And you think you're in love with me. We have bigger problems than trying to figure out a lesbian vampire romance right now."

"I do love you. You made me. Why do you have to put a label on it?"

"No, you're infatuated, there's a difference. And I didn't realize I was. I'm sorry for that."

"Don't tell me how I feel."

"I don't know how I made you, you know."

"I bit you."

"You remember that? I was so into ..."

"I do. I tasted you. It was intoxicating."

"I don't remember that, sweetie, I really don't."

And I really didn't. I didn't recall seeing a wound or a mark or anything.

"I saved your life. Twice. Isn't that worth something?"

"It is. But you and Julie were also about to kill a baby."

"God, we were so confused. We didn't know what the hell we were doing."

I kissed Sarah on the top of her head. "I know, honey. When we get to the other side of this mess, then we'll talk, okay? It's not over. I am gonna get a shower. Mind if I borrow something to wear when I get out?"

"Um, you sure you don't want to just burgle me again? Of course. I'll lay something out for you. I think I know what you like."

My hands slipped from her shoulders, and I shed my clothes as I made my way to the luxurious shower. I didn't expect Sarah to follow, but I wouldn't have turned her way if she had. I must admit I was a little disappointed when she didn't. It wasn't lost on me what had happened the last time I was in this shower. I would be lying if I said I hadn't enjoyed it.

I made the water as hot as I could stand, which was pretty fucking hot, and scrubbed the grime from my hair, limbs, and torso.

When I was finished scrubbing and toweling off, I found an outfit laid out on the bed. All I could do was chuckle. A pair of thigh-high patent-leather boots with stiletto heels sat on the floor near a black sleeveless turtleneck dress and a black patent-leather, three-quarter-length trench.

"What, no panties? No bra?" I called to the kitchen.

"Fuck you."

"Okay, then."

I got dressed, savoring each article and its feel against my skin. The boots were last and they slipped on with ease. I slid my hands up from the toe to the knee and made the shiny material squeak under the pressure. After zipping them up, I stood up and smoothed myself before walking back out to the kitchen. This was another one of those times when I wished I could see myself in a mirror. Something told me I was smoking hot.

Andrei and Sarah were sitting on stools at the breakfast bar. Andrei's face was devoid of expression but Sarah's jaw dropped. Maybe she wished she had joined me in the shower after all.

"Close your yap, Sarah, you're going to attract flies."

"Well, we're dead already, so ..."

"Ladies, enough. We have problems to discuss and solve. And yes, Elizabeth, you look stunning."

He was right. I had revenge on the brain, and I wasn't out for Andrei's head this time. Once again, he would have to wait. All this time I had been pursuing my maker wanting to end him for what he had done to me, and here he was just two feet away from me and I couldn't do a fucking thing about it. I needed him. And that pissed me off.

"I'm sorry about Julie."

"Thank you, Sarah."

Andrei opened his mouth to say something, and I just glared at him.

"Don't you say one fucking word about Julie."

He put his hands up in acquiescence. I reached across and grabbed him by the lapels and pulled him over the counter, bringing him nose-to-nose with me.

"Look, fucker, we still haven't addressed what you did to my brothers and their wives. I have this overwhelming desire to end you right the fuck now. But, unfortunately, I need your dumbass. If you so much as look at me sideways, I'll shove a stake so far up your ass it'll pop out of your heart from the inside. You got me?"

That twisted, depraved grin curled his lips.

"Of course, my dear."

I released Andrei. He straightened his jacket and stepped back out of arm's reach.

"We need to find Dietrich. I will not suffer a betrayal. You two I understand. What I don't get is people thinking they can cross me and get away with it. For some reason these yo-yos all think they're better off on the wrong side of the sadistic game of Red Rover. I have fucking had it. And Jonas of all people. Do either of you know why he would have switched sides here?"

Sarah just shrugged her shoulders and shook her head.

"Perhaps he didn't have to switch. Perhaps he was already playing for the other team."

I snapped my fingers and paced the kitchen.

"That makes some kind of sense. He never did really care for you after what you did, and it doesn't seem like he ever embraced what he is."

"How did you not know, Liz? Liz is okay, right?"

"Yes, Sarah. He never let on, and he was helping me at every turn. He pulled me out of the coal mine, and he ran interference the night I killed his old girlfriend."

"Was there a moment, was there anything that could have tripped his trigger?"

"I don't think he cared for me killing Christina, and I don't think he was fond of the fact I slept with someone the night after he and I …"

"Oh, for fuck's sake! You have got to be kidding. No wonder why he pulled the double cross."

Andrei interjected.

"No, I believe my original hypothesis is correct. Jonas was Ahura Mazda all along. I think he was disguised as a policeman for decades so he could help the Order track down and exterminate vampires. He wasn't just looking for me."

"So, he infiltrated the San Francisco Police Department. I wonder how he reconciled being a vampire with the Order. Lesser of two evils?"

"The enemy of my enemy is my friend," Sarah mused.

We were back to that on our side of the coin. That's the way I'd looked at what we'd had to do to dispatch Da Rocha. No wonder Jonas had been so reluctant to kill the

Order of Ahura Mazda's preeminent vampire slayer. How long would Jonas have lasted if we hadn't taken out Tobias and his thugs? Or maybe they had some kind of Faustian relationship. As long as you are of use, you get to live, once you outlive that usefulness, bang, a stake in the heart.

It was burning me up that I had to cozy up to Andrei. My entire family was dead because of him, directly or indirectly. I just wanted to pull a knife from the butcher block and drive it right through his rib cage. I absolutely hated the fucker.

"We need to find Dietrich. He knows where I sleep."

"Oh, this just keeps getting better."

"Sarah, enough. We've already established what an artful dodger Jonas Dietrich is. None of us knew."

My thoughts flashed to Whitney. Did Jonas kill her on purpose? Did she die because of me? Based on anecdotal evidence, I just couldn't buy that loss of control excuse anymore. How many times had I thought there was someone or something in my sanctuary? Could it have been Jonas all along? All of these bastards were responsible for the deaths of everyone I had ever cared about. The more I flipped this over in my head, the more I was convinced he had killed Whitney as a way to get at me, that it was part of some scheme.

"Well, we aren't going to find him tonight. Dawn comes. Sarah, Elizabeth is going to have to stay here with you. I'll help you prepare."

Andrei and Sarah made sure the makeshift blackout

curtains that were affixed to the rods in the master bedroom windows were secure. Thankfully those windows faced west and not east. I felt a little silly thinking I'd gotten dressed for nothing. Sarah never did change out of her bathrobe.

My jackass of a maker exited the house through the garage, and I chased after him. We stood in the driveway like two wild west gunslingers about to draw.

"You won't get off that easy, Andrei. When this is over, we're going to have more than words. One way or the other, we are going to end this."

"I'm sure you believe that, Elizabeth. But we shall cross that bridge when we come to it."

Before I could say another word, Andrei dissolved into mist and blew away on the night breeze.

I went back into the house, gave it the once over, and secured it. I found Sarah in bed. She had already pulled the bed clothes over her head. I quickly shed the outfit Sarah had meticulously assembled for me and climbed in with her. We were both naked and before long snuggled up nose to nose and chest to chest.

"You know this is only out of necessity, right?"

"Yes, honey."

Ever since our earlier conversation, I certainly felt more empathy for Sarah. Like Julie, she had never asked for any of this. She couldn't help how she felt. I was sure that she was just as confused as I had been. She nuzzled under my chin and cooed. I wrapped my arms around her and held her close. She was just as much a victim as Julie and I were.

Only in her case, I had been the predator. It was nice to have a little bit of clarity about what had happened. I still didn't know how or why Andrei's blood had ended up in my mouth that night. He did refer to me as a mistake. And Sarah was a legitimate accident in the throes of passion.

I kissed her on the forehead, and we were out.

CHAPTER XXI

When I arose to meet the night Sarah was already up and dressed. I peeled the covers to the side and stretched like I thought I needed to. Sarah was at the makeup table again, but this time she was dressed and her hair was dry.

I was still in a fog as I rolled over on to my stomach and turned my head in her direction.

"How long you been up?"

"Not long. Half hour maybe?"

"Sleep okay?"

"Like a rock. You?"

I was tempted to make some lame, cliché 'slept like the dead' wisecrack but thought better of it.

"Mmmhmmm. Andrei here yet?"

"No, but I suspect he'll be here sooner or later. You know he'll be fashionably late."

"He does have a flair for the dramatic."

"Do you dream?"

"Funny, I was going to ask you the same question. As a matter of fact, I don't. What about you?"

"No. I used to. I used to have such vivid dreams. It was almost like watching a movie in my head, you know? But now, well, everything is different now."

Her voice trailed off with the last few words of that sentence. I wondered how much of her fought for her humanity. She seemed to have embraced her new existence. With her devil-may-care attitude and sharp tongue, I found it hard to believe that she longed for her previous life.

"You ever miss it, being human, I mean?"

"Yeah, no, I guess there are some things I miss. It's really hard selling real estate like this. I miss the parties and mixers, the open houses. You can do the parties at night, but people get leery about evening open houses. They think you're trying to hide something. But I wouldn't trade what I can do or how I am for anything. You?"

Before I could answer the question, billowing white smoke erupted from the bedroom fireplace and filled the room. Within seconds, Andrei materialized. His transformations I never understood. You would think that you'd be able to see something, maybe bones first, then muscles and nerves, and then finally skin. But no. There was fog or mist and then poof, there was Andrei.

"Isn't this cozy?"

"You do know how to make an entrance, I'll give you that."

"Get dressed, Elizabeth, we have much to discuss. I know where Dietrich is."

With that, I flung the covers off and tried to hop off the bed. All I managed to do was roll off and land between the bed and the wall with an "ooof." After I righted myself, I put on the outfit from the night before. Sarah and I checked each other and made sure there wasn't a hair out of place as we headed for the kitchen and what I hoped to be a productive conversation with Andrei. I pounded down the hall ahead of Sarah and started formulating thoughts and questions before I got to the kitchen.

"Okay, Andrei, out with it, where is the fucker? And how the hell did you find out so fast?"

"Shhhhh." There was that finger to the lips again.

"I told you, don't shush me. I'll break that finger off and shove it up your nose. Now spill it, where is he?"

As Andrei explained and detailed where he believed Dietrich spent his days, I paced and shook my head. I knew the place all too well. It made too much sense. And it explained a lot. The crazy thing is I had sprung Dietrich from it once already. Now I was contemplating a commando raid of a police station. We were really going to go all *Assault on Precinct 13* here?

Andrei told us that Dietrich was using an antechamber below the police station to hide during the day. It also gave him all-hours access to the station and was a good jumping-off point for his investigations. According to my maker, tunnels led to Mission Rock Street and China Basin Street and Terry A Francois Boulevard along the water.

I stopped my pacing long enough to ask, "How in the hell do you find this stuff out?"

Sarah was stunned with Andrei's wealth of knowledge.

"Yeah, seriously, Andrei, you keep coming up with some CIA-level shit here."

"You know I broke him out of there once, right? I am sure they tightened their security protocols since then. I highly doubt that we're going to be able to waltz in there and dispatch the thing in the basement that easily."

"Elizabeth, you're overreacting. I am not suggesting we lay siege or even try to infiltrate the building. You are correct in that it is as secure as a fortress. Despite our considerable abilities and invisibility to security cameras, such an undertaking would be suicide. And in case you hadn't noticed, I am rather fond of *living*."

"Fair enough. Then what are you suggesting?"

"We draw him out and then use the tunnel he emerges from to slip inside his sanctuary. When he returns, we destroy him."

"You really think that bullshit is going to work?"

"Sarah, it sounds like a decent idea. One worth exploring, at least. We should do some recon of the area, verify Andrei's information, and see if we can establish some sort of pattern of movement."

"That makes more sense than just playing sewer rat without corroborating this information."

Huh. I showed Sarah a little bit of kindness, and now all of a sudden she was on team Elizabeth? I wasn't going to complain, but I also wasn't going to count on her staying that way. Her moods and loyalties seemed to change with the wind.

"Okay, it's settled. We'll head over to 3rd Street and take up positions near the police station. Before the night is through, hopefully we'll have a read on Dietrich. And after a couple of nights we'll have a pattern, then I'm going to staple the fucker to the back of his coffin."

We left Sarah's house and started to stroll down the street. Within a few steps, Andrei blended into the fog, and Sarah and I had taken wing. The thirty-mile flight north was agonizing and slow. It was better than driving, I suppose. I didn't care for bright headlights and from what I could see below, traffic was a bitch tonight. A little bit of a headwind wasn't such a problem after all. It was the crosswind I was having trouble with.

Sarah and I put in at Bay Front Park. I figured it was a safe distance from the police station, and Andrei would be able to just roll in off the water. Right on cue a fog bank crept along the coast and drifted to our position. Andrei stepped out of the mist as if he were disembarking from a yacht. He was dressed as we'd last seen him just over thirty minutes earlier with one exception. He wasn't wearing shoes. I was never going to get over his claw-like feet. They were disgusting and disturbing.

We approached from the San Francisco Bay Trail, which merged into Terry A Francois Boulevard. Sarah was to continue north to Mission Rock Street, Andrei to China Basin, and I was going to make a left on Mission Bay Boulevard North and break right on Bridgeview Way. A few businesses dotted the block. I just didn't think Dietrich would be brazen enough to try to exit via 3rd. He was a fugitive for fuck's sake, and he was hiding right under their noses. There was no way he had squared things with SFPD. As much as Ahura Mazda was able to cover up Tim's murder, Dietrich aiding and abetting a serial killer was something they just wouldn't overlook.

Andrei said that one of the tunnels exited near the fire station on Mission Rock, one at the Mariposa Hunters Point Yacht Club, and another at Mission Bay Commons Park. We were strategically placed to catch at least a glimpse of our trench coat-wearing turncoat. The plan was to meet back at Bay Front Park at four o'clock. That would give me and Sarah time to fly back to her house, and Andrei could, well, do whatever Andrei did.

I was getting thirsty.

I never did see Dietrich, and I trudged back to the rendezvous. Sarah had, however. Andrei and I listened as she recalled what she saw.

"Fuck, it was just about a half an hour ago. I was going to head back here a little early. I was ready to give up. I felt really exposed with my back to that empty parking lot but I managed to scoot over to the fire station before he could see me. He came from Pier 50. Then he used the tunnel on the east side of the fire house."

"You sure he didn't see you?"

Sarah shot Andrei a middle school "duh" glare.

"Okay, thanks, Sarah. We have to make sure we stick things out. We all keep very strange hours. Obviously, Dietrich does too."

"Well done, Sarah. Meet back here tomorrow night?"

"Yeah, Andrei, no need to meet at Sarah's first; we know what we need to do."

Andrei drifted off into the fog just off the spit.

"Why doesn't the water bother him, Liz?"

"I don't know, baby, I don't know."

We sprinted a few steps and transformed. The flight back was a bit more leisurely, and the wind had died down. Sarah and I arrived back at her house just short of 5:30 a.m. We went inside and disrobed. It didn't take long for us to fall asleep once we'd snuggled up in the darkness of our makeshift sanctuary.

For the next two nights, we repeated the exercise. Each time a different one of us saw Dietrich, but it was always at the same time. We never did see him leave, but we watched him return. Before we parted company that third morning, Andrei was ready to strike.

"We have his pattern, we have his routine. Tomorrow night, he'll come by way of the firehouse."

"No, this is too easy," I said. "Look at what Tobias did. You can't tell me that wasn't a setup, taking coffee at the same time each night at the same spot. Dietrich is of them, right? So he would know how to set up a faux routine. Hell, that's how I got my clock cleaned."

"Elizabeth is right, Andrei, this stinks."

"Either he knows the three of us are watching him and he made sure he was visible to all three of us, or he is laying the groundwork for some kind of trap. We need more intel. Andrei's information only seems to come in bursts."

"If you don't want my help, just say so."

"No, sorry. I just think this is all way too convenient."

"You've made your point. What would you like us to do?"

Again, why in the hell was I in charge of this operation? Dietrich and Ahura Mazda, if there was any of it left, were as big a threat to them as they were to me. Why didn't either one of them take command? I guess I could complain, but neither one of them would listen. I'd rather make the decisions that affected my well-being, I suppose.

We spent the next nine nights tracking Jonas, mapping his tunnel usage and his approaches. He changed every three days, reversing the pattern every fourth night. Sarah and I hunted and fed on the locals nearby. We enjoyed couples taking romantic strolls, the occasional homeless guy, the late night Starbucks barista. Some tried to run. None escaped. Each morning, we retired to the darkness of

Sarah's bedroom with the blackout curtains, the covers over our heads, and our arms around each other.

Dietrich was like clockwork; there wasn't a night when one of us didn't see him. That's what worried me. We were going to have to flip the script on him. I knew he was planning something for us The itch in the back of my brain told me that. I had an idea, and Sarah wasn't going to like it.

CHAPTER XXII

"Okay, gang. We need a plan to take Dietrich down. He knows we're coming, he just doesn't know when."

"How do you know this, Elizabeth?"

"Trust me, Andrei. He's been setting us up this whole time. So, I have an idea. We never see him leave, but we always see him come back, so the one thing that I think it is safe to assume is that he leaves a different way but that he does leave every night. Sarah, you're not going to like this."

She rolled her eyes and crossed her arms.

"Andrei, you are to keep the cops out of the basement or antechamber or whatever the hell it is. Hopefully, all you'll have to do is be the lookout. Sarah … you're going to be the bait."

"Goddammit."

"We aren't going to have much time to do this. I want you to make yourself very visible a bit before four o'clock. Make sure he sees you. He'll follow you into the tunnel to his lair. I'll follow behind. Once we're in his sanctuary, we take him. Andrei, if it all goes sideways, you come a-running."

"What do you propose, Elizabeth, would you like me to get myself arrested?"

"You know what? I really don't give a fuck what you do. Just keep the police off our necks."

He bowed with a theatrical flourish, and Sarah rolled her eyes again.

We took up our positions and waited. And waited. And waited.

What I didn't tell my little squad was that I planned to employ some backup. I closed my eyes and reached out for the nearest colony of bats. Something *shifted*, and I made a mental connection with a swarm near Lake Merced Rim. I scrambled them and willed them to my location. It wouldn't take them long to flap their way across the city. I needed an advantage, and I hoped my winged friends would give it to me.

Dietrich was late, and I knew we'd be racing the sunset. I also worried that there might be a fire call. The last thing we needed was the fire trucks to have to roll as we were in the middle of our operation. The bats had been circling for a while, and I saw Dietrich before Sarah did. She did as instructed and waited until he saw her before darting toward the tunnel entrance near the firehouse.

She flung the heavy metal doors open as if she were running from a Kansas twister. She closed them behind her and was careful not to wake up the San Francisco Fire Department. Dietrich quickened his pace when he saw Sarah and where she was heading. He was hot on her heels and not far behind her when she made it to the tunnel. His mistake was not closing the doors behind him.

I commanded the bats to follow. They swirled and dived for the firehouse. The bats made a swirling vortex of themselves as they blasted their way through the opening. Andrei stood on the roof of the fire station watching with his mouth agape.

Strutting down the street toward my destination, I saw as the bats saw and viewed a long passageway. It was narrow, and I could only see Dietrich's trench coat. My coat billowed behind me like a cape. Sarah was nowhere in sight. My view was obscured by the detective. Wall sconces lit the way along the passage.

The tunnel opened into a void. A coffin, an ornate, onyx coffin with gold trim and accents sat atop a stone pedestal. Sconces were evenly placed around the space, bathing it in firelight. I finally spotted Sarah. She was in the corner, her back pressed up against the wall, and she was covering her ears to shield them from the shrieking of the bats. The noise reverberated off the walls and distracted Dietrich.

As I followed, I removed one of the sconces from its wall

brackets. I found my way into the void. Dietrich was staring at Sarah. Her eyes gave me away as she glanced in my direction. He spun around just as the bats flew out into the passage from whence we came.

"Sorry, Jonas."

I swung the sconce at his head like a baseball bat, and he dropped like a rock on contact. I didn't give him a chance to regain consciousness. I straddled him with one foot on either side of him at the waist. After one tentative blow, I bashed his skull in with the sconce. Ember and flame swirled like demon fire as I raised the sconce over my head like a battle axe and brought the torch down blow after blow. Each strike was harder than the last. The sound was sickening. It was a wet, squishy sound mixed with the crunching of bone. The last thing Jonas's dead eyes saw were my patent-leather boots.

Sarah was frozen to her spot. I could see from the look on her face she was terrified ... of me. "W-w-w-what did you just do? Oh, my God, Elizabeth, what the fuck did you just do?"

I grabbed her by the wrist and dragged her toward the passageway. The sounds of a commotion started to rise, and I had the sinking feeling that cops were closing in from one of the other tunnels.

"COME ON! We need to go." She wouldn't budge, and she looked like she was going to cry. I softened my tone. "C'mon, baby, I won't hurt you. But we gotta go, now." She shifted in her spot, and I took that as my cue.

I dragged Sarah behind me, her shoulders bouncing off the walls as we hurried along. She was still stunned and frightened. We sprinted up the four steps of the entryway and burst into the night air. The telltale sound of jackboots, leather, and weapons weren't far behind. I commanded the bats to return. They swirled and zoomed back down into the tunnel entrance and engaged the cops. Screaming was followed by semiautomatic gunfire.

Sarah and I stood outside the firehouse, not sure which way to turn or run.

"Some plan; you really didn't think this out, did ya?"

"Shut up, Sarah, let me think."

Before I could form a thought or even an inkling, we were enveloped in fog or mist and carried away. I could've sworn I saw Andrei's smug, smiling face in the cloud as we were whisked along on the wind. We rolled across the peninsula and skirted the coast as we made our way south past South San Francisco, San Bruno, Millbrae, Burlingame, Foster City, and Bair Island. I had no idea what was keeping us afloat, and I was stunned by how fast we moved.

The sun was just starting to creep over the horizon.

We emerged from the fog near Sarah's house. *"Go …"* And we went. The two of us sprinted for the house and made it under the comforter just in time. No time to undress. I planted a gentle kiss on Sarah's nose as sleep took us.

CHAPTER XXIII

I awakened before Sarah this time. I gently peeled the thick, heavy comforter back and slipped out. Stripping my clothes off piece by piece, I made my way to the shower. The water heated up quickly, and I was eager to let it cascade all over me from head to toe. The shampoo lathered and within a few seconds of scrubbing my hair and scalp, I could see blood and bits of what could only be skull flowing down in rivulets along the curves of my breasts, stomach, and legs. I really didn't care.

This shower was going to wash away a lot of things and in a way, it was a bit of a rebirth. Sure, I had some unfinished business. But I felt like I had shed some dead skin, and I was about to emerge shiny and new.

Jonas had to go. I didn't regret killing him in the least. Maybe I should have given him a few seconds to try to explain. It wasn't him that I didn't trust in that moment, it was me. I just knew that if I had given him the opportunity to speak, I would have let him off the hook. And after what he'd done to me, he didn't deserve to be.

I don't know if you've noticed, but I don't take too kindly to betrayals.

What I really needed to know was what had made Jonas do it. Why was he with Ahura Mazda? If he was a vampire, why didn't they end him? Circumstantial and direct evidence was going to be a lot better than whatever song-and-dance bullshit anecdotal evidence he would have provided with a wall sconce aimed at his head. People about to die will say anything. I would know.

While I was contemplating and ruminating over the events of the past week and a half, I didn't notice Sarah slip into the shower with me. I half turned to see the look on her face. It was sheepish, tentative. She was still afraid of me. "Oh, baby, don't be frightened. I'm not going to hurt you."

"Is it okay that I'm in here with you?"

I thought about that for moment, remembering the last time Sarah and I had shared this shower.

"Of course it is."

Before I could turn around to face her, she was scrubbing my back with a sponge loofah. She ran it across my neck and shoulders and down my spine to the crack of my ass. Then guided it between my legs. I parted them to give her better access. She reached down and washed my legs and the tops of my feet, all while I had my back to her.

I spun around as she stood up and took her face in my hands. I kissed her full on the mouth, my tongue pushing her teeth apart and finding hers. My hands raced over her and within seconds they were full of hot water, soap, and Sarah's breasts. I bent down and took a nipple in my mouth and bit down hard. She shrieked with ecstasy, and she tipped her head and arched her back, pushing her breast into my face. My hand slid down her flat stomach and found her sex. She gasped and rode my fingers as I inserted them.

Then I turned her around and pressed my chest against her back. I filled my hands with her breasts again and pinched her nipples. As I reached down and fingered her, my fangs extended, and I sank them deep into the meat of her shoulder. The deepest groan emitted from her throat as she came.

A black motor oil-like substance oozed from the wound as my fangs and mouth retracted. I cleaned Sarah off, as the bite had already begun to heal, and suggested we continue in the bed. We didn't even towel off, and I don't even know which one of us killed the water. I didn't care. We tumbled into bed and made love for what seemed like hours.

After our marathon session, we drifted off for a bit. I snapped awake. I had an idea. I raided Sarah's closet for some clothes and got dressed. Nothing fancy, just a pair of jeans, a turtleneck, an overcoat, and a pair of running shoes. Just as I was tying the trainers, Sarah emerged from her dozing.

"Where are you going?"

"Don't worry. I have something I need to do. I won't be long."

"I'm thirsty, I need to feed."

"I know, baby. I'll try to bring you someone." That was a lie.

"I love you."

I didn't reciprocate, and I dashed out of Sarah's house and took flight. It took almost forty-five minutes to get to Jones Street, and another fifteen to break into apartment 409. I was still surprised SFPD hadn't found this place yet, but Dietrich must have covered his tracks very well. It was as we had left it. Apparently, Dietrich had been using the sanctuary under the police station almost exclusively. Sarah and I hadn't had time to conduct a thorough search of the place, but it didn't look like there were any papers or documents, or even anything that might contain such things.

The apartment was dank and musty. I really didn't know what I was looking for. It was kinda like I'd know it when I saw it. I started rifling through the drawers, the cupboards, the dressers, the oven. From room to room I went, and I left no door unopened, no mattress or pillow unturned. I found my way back to the kitchen and just stood there tapping my foot. The sneakers were taking some getting used to, as I expected the sound of stiletto heels hitting the floor, not rubber. Annoyed because I couldn't find what I was looking for, annoyed because I couldn't stomp my foot the way I wanted to, I went back to the drawers and fished out a screwdriver. I thought, maybe, just maybe, there might be a box or a safe hidden in an air duct or a vent. How the hell did my life become a Coen brothers movie?

I went back to what was Jonas's bedroom and tore the closet apart. There was a shoebox full of old snapshots. His family, I supposed. I really wasn't in the mood to get all nostalgic. I wanted to find something that would link Dietrich to the Order of Ahura Mazda and try to understand why the bastard had betrayed me.

The expression, "I found it, it was in the last place I looked," has to be one of the most inane things ever. Of course it was in the last place you looked. There is no need to look anywhere else. Well, I found Dietrich's box of goodies in the last place I looked. I got lucky, really. I was just about to give up; I was done. Dietrich's wife's dresser beckoned and begged for another look. It was as if I had opened a time capsule. You would have thought I'd stepped through a portal to the 1940s. I tossed panties and girdles and bras and slips. Not finding anything right away, I put my hands on my hips and huffed.

For some reason I was convinced that this was where Dietrich would have hidden his secrets. He wouldn't be tempted to pull this stuff out very often lest he disturb the memory of his dead wife. I started pulling the drawers out. Nothing. Except ... one of the drawers seemed to be shallower than the others. I wasn't in the mood, and I didn't care about preserving the heirloom-quality furniture.

I tore the drawer apart.

Six passports, a rubber band-bound roll of cash, a minicassette recorder, and a weathered dark brown portfolio fell to the carpet. This sure didn't look like cop shit, it looked like spy shit. I flipped open the passports. The photos were all Jonas, but the names weren't "Jonas Dietrich." I thumbed the wad of bills, all twenty-dollar bills. I didn't give a damn about any of this stuff; I needed to see what was in that portfolio.

I bent down and picked it up. After sweeping the top of the dresser clear with my arm, I opened what proved to be a dossier of some kind. It was full of loose papers and documents that were clipped in place. Familiar-looking biographical sketches like the one he'd left for me about Andrei. Were these vampires that he had hunted or helped Ahura Mazda destroy? Was his story about his wife a lie? Considering that he had played me for a fool, I doubted everything he had ever told me.

While I flipped through, a sheet caught my eye. My name at the top. His distinctive handwriting.

Elizabeth Danae Rubis—Age 44—female

June 22, 2018

Rubis is new and raw. She exhibits the traits of a spree killer or mass murderer, not methodical like others of her kind. No discretion. Highly intelligent, but extremely impulsive and dangerous. I have been able to gain her trust through a series of staged events, or by inserting myself into life-threatening situations.

I couldn't read anymore. Fucker. He'd played me for a sucker all along. But why? And what staged events? I kept flipping. A yellowed, decaying letter-sized envelope fell out. Jesus Christ. I picked that up. I pulled out what could only be described as a piece of parchment. I opened the fragile document. It was a contract of some kind. I saw the bottom and the signatures first. Tobias and Dietrich. Figures. When I looked above the top fold, I saw the date—1948.

Jonas had entered into this agreement to keep Ahura Mazda from killing him. He agreed to help them track down and destroy vampires. In exchange, they let him live. Goddammit. I felt like such a fool. I wondered if he meant what he said in that note he left me, "I could've fallen for you," or whatever the fucker had written. Was that bullshit too? How many times had he saved my bacon? For what? He could have finished me or made sure that I was done for numerous times, but each time he pulled my butt out of the fire. Maybe he really did care. Maybe he was conflicted and dragged out my execution. Maybe he was just a dead double-crossing bastard vampire detective with his skull bashed in.

I took the bedroom apart. I screamed so loud the paint should have melted off the walls. All I got was a low rumble of thunder and some raindrops on the window. By the time I was done with Jonas's secret apartment, the furniture was in pieces, the bedclothes and curtains where in shreds, and I was sobbing on the floor. Well, as much as I could sob.

I flew back to Sarah's in a steady drizzle. It was an agonizing, emotional flight, and I had trouble flying straight. All this time I'd thought Andrei was my nemesis, my archenemy, the one I needed to vanquish. All along, it was Dietrich. I wondered how long it would have taken him to get around to me if I hadn't sought him out first.

A wayward flock of pelicans snapped me out of my distracted flying. They almost knocked me out of the sky. Nasty birds. It took me much longer to get back to Sarah's than I would have liked. When I landed and transformed, I was angry, hurt, and wet.

I made a pit stop in the kitchen on the way to the bedroom, where I found Sarah still naked in bed. She was in a dreamlike state, and not in a good way. The thirst had her.

"Did you bring me anything? Or anyone?"

"No, baby. It's been a bad night."

"But I'm thirsty," she whined.

"I know, honey."

"W-w-what happened?"

I peeled the clothes from my body as I explained what I'd found at Dietrich's apartment.

"So, yeah, our little detective friend turned out to be a real dick."

"What an asshole. You fucked him, didn't you?"

"Yeah, not the first colossal mistake I ever made."

When I was sufficiently nude, I climbed into bed with Sarah. She didn't notice the item I had brought with me from the kitchen even as I slid it under my pillow.

"Kiss me, Elizabeth, please."

I rolled on top of her and kissed her deeply. Our lips locked. Her hips rose to meet me as she arched. She threw her arms around me and pulled me tight and close. I felt my hips press against her inner thighs. We kissed and caressed. She had gone from an angry, bitter jilted lover to needy and clingy overnight. Maybe I had been wrong to show her that kindness. Maybe I was wrong to have tried to be sympathetic. It really didn't matter. She was an accident, a mistake, and as much fun as the sex was, I couldn't move on until I'd rectified it.

I used my body weight to press her into the mattress as I reached under the pillow and pulled out a large butcher's knife. I broke the kiss and grabbed the knife by the handle with two hands. I raised it up high over my head. Sarah opened her eyelids just before I plunged the blade deep into her chest. The look on her face almost made me stop. Almost.

"Sorry, baby, you were never meant to be."

The knife hit her flesh with a thud, slipped between her ribs, and found its mark. You'd think I would have stopped there, but you would be wrong. Dead wrong. I destroyed Sarah's torso with that knife. Blow after blow. Strike after strike. Her head lolled to the side, her rib cage was caved in, and black vampire blood goo was everywhere. And I was in a delightful homicidal rage. How many times had I fought these primal urges, held back because I didn't understand what I was? Or was it my humanity hanging on for dear life? Maybe it was just as simple as just taking my anger about Jonas out on Sarah. Well, I did feel a tremendous relief or release when the light left Sarah's eyes.

I had made way too many mistakes learning my existence and my new place in the world, and I was determined to atone for them. The vampire I accidently created had to go. If it had been my choice, I would have turned Whitney. But I didn't get that opportunity, now, did I?

After coming down from my murderous high, I dragged Sarah's lifeless, mangled body to the garage. Naked and crazed, I searched the space for something with which I could remove her head. Did this bitch really not own a reciprocating saw? No circular saw, no jigsaw? I went back to the kitchen. Well, at least she had an electric knife.

I went back to the garage, plugged in the appliance, and proceeded to saw her head off. Sarah's noggin made a "thunk" sound when I dropped it in the kitchen garbage can.

I took a slow walk back to the master bedroom. My sharp nails dragged across the walls, taking paint and wallpaper with them. Jagged claw marks were left in my wake. Despite my discoveries earlier in the evening, I felt deliciously evil.

The shower called to me and I obliged. The hot water and soap were delightful on my skin. I shampooed my hair, scrubbed my arms and legs, used that sponge loofah on my back, legs, and feet. No blood. Just Sarah's viscous, black liquid. Now her life really swirled down the drain, for the last time, for good.

I still wasn't sure how it worked or why, but I reached down between my legs and brought myself to orgasm with a little help from the handheld shower attachment. My back hit the wall, and I slid down until my ass hit the floor. The water cascaded over me from the top of my head down my chest and stomach to my sex. I just let it wash over me.

Everything played out on a movie screen in my mind. The Dark Truth, the night Andrei took me, the boutique massacre, little Emily, Billy, the diner owner, Julie, Jonas, Sarah, Ahura Mazda, Tobias, my brothers and their wives, transforming into various creatures, my murderous rage, all of it …

It all went down the drain. Everything. I imagined the water just pulling all of these things out of me. It was the most amazing shower.

I got out and toweled myself off. I strutted around Sarah's house naked. I made sure that it was secure, and I really didn't care about her headless body lying on the garage floor. I went back to the bedroom and hunkered down after changing the sheets and comforter on the bed. I wasn't sure where the knife was. The bed was comfortable and cozy, and I stretched out since I didn't have to share it with anyone. I threw the heavy bedclothes over my head, and one more thought crept into my brain.

I had one more thing to do.

CHAPTER XXIV

Andrei.

I actually had a dream. I couldn't tell you the last time I'd had one. It was more like a day-mare. Every moment, every second, every encounter I'd had or thought I'd had with Andrei flashed through my mind. The face in the window, that night in my bedroom when I was a kid, my last night as a human being. The dream lingered on my murder. I was trussed up on that giant wooden X, naked and bleeding from multiple wounds.

I tried to pay attention to the details. Maybe this wasn't a dream, maybe these were repressed memories straining to break free from my subconscious. My vision blurred and I squinted, but I couldn't see. Andrei's wrist was in his mouth. And then the taste was in my own mouth.

He made me.

I wasn't an accident after all. I wasn't a mistake. He made me on purpose. But why? And why did he reject me? Or was that a consideration at all? Why me? Why not any of the others?

Maybe he just wanted a windup toy he could set loose on the city to throw the authorities off his trail. As much as he'd tried to warn me to control my feeding habits and keep a low profile, maybe I was his weapon. This would explain why he acquiesced each time we needed him to join the fray against our common enemies.

One of the most annoying things about my time as a vampire had to be the lack of answers. I always seemed to have more questions. Each time I'd knock one down, several more popped up.

Before I could actually see my lips clamped down on Andrei's wrist in my dream, I sat bolt upright, awake. My arms plopped on top of the rumpled covers, and I felt like I had just woken up from a three-day bender. Had I my original locks, I'm sure I would've looked like I had gotten my head stuck in a blender. In that case, I was glad my hair was closely cropped.

My eyesight sharpened and adjusted. The evidence from what I had done to Sarah was all over the place. Her motor oil-like blood was splattered all over the walls and even on the ceiling. No remorse. No regrets. I chuckled at the thought of a crime scene clean-up crew coming in here and trying to scrub Sarah off the dual-propeller ceiling fan. How long would it take CSI to find her head in the trash? Probably faster than it was going to take me to find Andrei, but hey, the thought of them rummaging around and coming across her decomposing cranium in a Hefty bag made me laugh.

The only people I was truly going to miss were Julie and my brothers. I did feel sick about dragging Julie into all of this, and she'd died twice. Twice. My brothers and their wives didn't deserve any of what had happened to them, and I blamed Tobias for that. He'd used them as bait. He'd paid for that and a lot of other things with his life, as had his whole fucking crew.

I wondered what would happen to my parents' estate now. My nieces and nephews were too young to inherit anything. They'd get everything when they turned eighteen, I supposed. There was a trip to Livermore in my near future. I needed to see what was happening in the neighborhood and what had happened with Ahura Mazda's vehicles and equipment. Plus, there was the aftermath of Andrei's killing spree inside the house to consider.

Since Tobias and Ahura Mazda had wielded so much influence over the local authorities, I wondered how Livermore PD was going to handle this. Maybe Ahura Mazda wasn't as finished as I thought, and they were cleaning up their own mess. Whatever the case may be, I needed to make my way there to find out.

Yeah. Now would be good. Andrei would wait. Seriously. He wasn't going anywhere. Even when we all were supposed to break off and go our separate ways, Andrei had never left the area. That made me wonder if he was bound to a burial place. It made sense. We vampires were supposed to have to rest in our native soil. Since I'd never been interred, I didn't have to. I just needed absolute darkness. My body had become attuned to sunrise and sunset. My sleep was like death with one startling exception, that I woke up and was ambulatory after sundown each day. That deathlike sleep was unique in one other way—no dreams—now with one startling exception—those memories of Andrei that had come flooding back during my most recent slumber. I wondered if I would dream again.

On to Livermore. I dressed in my favorite outfit and headed out. After walking a few blocks, I sprinted into a transformation and flapped off. It was roughly a thirty-mile flight. I followed Route 84 this time, and the Dumbarton Bridge gave me pause. I wondered if I would ever lose this fear of bodies of water. I managed to cut some time by cutting across as the bat flies rather than following the freeways. This also gave my eyes a break and kept me from wanting to count every car's headlights that zipped by below me.

Max Baer Park was deserted. I flew in low and transformed into a strut. Several emergency vehicles were parked along Fluorite Court and Tourmaline Avenue. Police cars, a couple of ambulances, and the coroner's car were parked along the street. A single wrecker was towing away what looked to be the last of Ahura Mazda's support vehicles. Yellow police tape was everywhere, as were uniformed and plainclothes officers. But it looked like much of the heavy lifting had been done. I did see the telltale flashes as crime scene technicians photographed the interior of the house.

It was my belief that if Ahura Mazda had still been a thing, I would not have witnessed what I just had. This would have been cleaned up quickly and quietly, not publicly. It was still hard to believe that this ancient order of vampire slayers was no more. Maybe Andrei had been right, maybe they had been a shell of their former selves when we'd come up against them in recent days. I wasn't so sure.

The scene in front of me was surreal but also all too familiar. It was Tobias and his gang of mercenaries before, and now it was the cops. Either way, armed goons were making a mess of my parents' house. Thankfully, I had not had the occasion to come back and witness the cleanup after I'd murdered my folks. But I had seen my brothers there during the aftermath, back when they thought my body had been stolen. They died thinking or even knowing that their sister was a monster.

I thought about channeling a bumblebee bat for surveillance but ultimately decided that it wasn't worth it. What could I possibly learn that I didn't know already? I'd told Andrei back at Sarah's that night that his time was coming. His fucking time was now.

That night I'd met Jack in Alameda, I'd seen a billboard that struck me as odd. Now it was serving as inspiration for Andrei's demise. I flew to the Bayshore Roundhouse. I didn't exactly feel comfortable at Sarah's anymore. I would have been tempted to clean the place. The abandoned rail yard had been the perfect sanctuary. I hadn't wanted to give it up, but I didn't have much choice at the time. Enough time had passed that it should serve me well again.

It took more than an hour to get there, and nature had taken more of it back. It didn't take me long to find my boxcar. I walked around it several times feeling nostalgic. Billy and I had spent many a day in that boxcar; we had been confronted by Andrei in that boxcar, and graffiti artists had made for an easy meal. Things were coming full circle. All of my enemies, save one, had been eliminated. And I had a plan for that asshole. I was back in a familiar hiding place, and I had nothing but time.

There had been many times that I'd thought I wasn't alone. All too many times I'd thought my sanctuary had been infiltrated. But it was the boxcar here at Bayshore in which Andrei had magically appeared that night. My gut told me that the creeper had been Jonas. It made perfect sense. He'd followed me, observed me, and reported back to Tobias or whoever his handler was. I couldn't imagine that there was some deranged ghoul out there in additional to us little ol' vampires. But hey, not that long ago I didn't think there were such things as vampires. So, there you go.

As you might have guessed, that one thing I had left to

do was to rid the world of Andrei. I didn't know how many vampires walked the earth, and I really didn't give a fuck. They could live out their eternities or walk into broad daylight for all I cared. There was only one I was concerned with, and we would all be better off without him.

My disdain for Andrei had done nothing but grow by leaps and bounds over time. Perhaps some vampires had a connection with or an affinity for their maker. I was not one of those vampires.

His list of crimes against humanity was one thing; his rap sheet when it came to the Rubis family was another matter. What made it worse was the knowledge that he had been stalking me since I was twelve. He had killed me, which in turn had led to the deaths of my parents, and murdered my brothers and my sisters-in-law when he was supposed to be helping eradicate the Order of Ahura Mazda.

What still burned was the night he'd turned me. Aside from those occasions when Andrei had peeped in my windows or the one time I know of that he'd snuck into my bedroom, I had never been sexually assaulted by anyone ever. I had been lucky in that regard, I suppose. None of my dates or boyfriends had ever gotten overly aggressive or ever touched me inappropriately or violently. But Andrei. He'd violated me. He'd violated me in ways I didn't even know were possible. The voyeurism, the breaking and entering, the kidnapping, binding and biting me, making me drink his blood—all violations.

I spent the rest of the night with my thoughts alternating between all the times Andrei and I may have crossed paths and how I was going to catch him and kill him. My deliciously creative idea on how to end him floated across my mind as sleep came for me.

CHAPTER XXV

I did not dream this time, and I was thankful for that. My repressed memories had told me all I needed to know. The shocking revelations illuminated details of the night I was murdered. What should not have shocked me was finding Blackfoot in the boxcar with me when I awakened. She curled up in my lap, and I gave her a good long scratch.

"You saved my life, you little bitch. You know that? Of course you do."

Blackfoot just nuzzled and purred in response. I still didn't know what to make of the fuzzball. All that time living with me and she'd had me on the pay-no-mind list except when it was feeding time. Then I become this ... thing ... and all of a sudden, we're best pals. I really shouldn't complain, especially after what she'd done to Tobias. From what I had seen prior to that, I didn't know the little shit had it in her.

It was only a matter of time before my children of the night found me again. I was looking forward to being surrounded by bats, spiders, mice, rats, and all manner of nocturnal creatures. It hadn't been easy for them to find me on Alcatraz. Oh, a few arachnids did, a mouse or two, but nothing like the abandoned church. Frankly, I missed the bats more than anything. Now that they were all my friends, I did feel bad about the raccoons in the coal mine. Had I known about my abilities then, I might have been able to use them as allies. But then again, they did attack my cat.

Maybe that's what it was. Blackfoot had paid me back for saving her from the raccoons, that's why she'd shredded Tobias's face.

While I was waxing nostalgic about the abandoned cathedral, I thought about my push pins and strings and map. All the trappings of playing detective to find Andrei the last time. I wasn't going to need them now. I had a pretty good idea how I was going to finish him. But I had to find him first. Then I would have to draw him out and lure him to the killing ground. Finding Da Rocha was what had brought him out before; it wasn't going to be that easy.

And what if the fucker had gone underground? What if he'd moved on and found new territory? The former was more likely than the latter. He'd settled in San Francisco when he made landfall in the United States and stayed. Sure, he may have traveled, but the Bay Area was home, and it had been for more than one hundred years.

It was time to go back to the newspapers, TV, and online reporting. He may have changed things up a bit in recent weeks so he could concentrate on Ahura Mazda, but he was a creature of habit and had a distinct MO. He would most certainly go back to his old ways. That meant Andrei would be on the radar of local law enforcement, and the manhunt would be on again.

Had I been thinking straight at the time, I would have searched Dietrich's apartment for any information he might have had on Andrei, his old case files, documents. There was no way I could go back there now. I all but lit a match to the place, and I figured that the SFPD would discover the clandestine real estate holding if they continued to investigate him.

There was some thought that Andrei's resting place might be near the Ferry Building. That's what Billy had thought when he was tailing Dietrich for me when I'd first claimed the kid at the Dark Truth. We'd had him cornered by the police at that abandoned warehouse, but he'd gotten away. He'd killed women as far south as Monterey and as far north as Mendocino. He never did seem to venture inland; he always stuck to the coast. I knew his type. But that wasn't going to help me. How many dark, curly-haired women with green eyes and a similar complexion to mine were there? Probably fewer than I thought, but too many to try to narrow down the next victim, especially without sophisticated database technology. Hell, the DMV could probably help, but I didn't exactly have access.

It was time to get somewhere and starting browsing the news. An old familiar haunt would suffice. I let Blackfoot out, secured my boxcar, and headed for that twenty-four-hour Starbucks. I decided to walk. It was a long stroll, but a familiar one, and I had missed it. Nothing remarkable, not much by way of scenery, but it had served as my conduit from the rail yard to The City on many a night, and it felt good to tread on terrain I knew well.

It took about an hour to walk to the coffee shop. I was in no hurry. Blackfoot followed along for a while before peeling off to find a morsel. I ordered a coffee, found my way to a back booth I knew all too well, and pulled out my smart phone.

"Okay, fucker, let's see what you've been up to."

It didn't take me long to find some promising headlines, but I ruled them out quickly. It was fascinating to read that a couple of serial killers who had been hunted for decades had finally been caught thanks to new DNA techniques. Unfortunately, all too many local rags had gone out of business or had been swallowed up by some large publishing conglomerate. So, coverage might be hard to find if Andrei was prowling the smaller coastal towns.

The *Napa Valley Register* had this, though ...

"The Napa Police Department is asking for any tips from residents as they investigate a bizarre alleged murder. A local business owner, 46-year-old Elektra Mellas, was found crucified at the edge of Skyline Wilderness Park just southeast of Napa.

Mellas was discovered by an elderly couple walking their dog along the north side of the park along Imola Avenue. Police have declined to speculate on the cause of death pending an autopsy. It is believed, however, that this case may be connected to several Bay Area slayings that have taken place over the past 18 months."

A photo of Mellas accompanied the story. She could have been my sister. That didn't take long. That date on the story was yesterday. He must have had her picked out already. Andrei probably figured Napa would be good. It was sufficiently far enough away from San Francisco, but still convenient to get to.

Several Sacramento TV stations had picked up the story and posted footage to their websites. Blurry video of the park shot at a distance revealed a giant wooden X, and you could just make out Mellas's silhouette hanging from it. The fucker was consistent, I'll give him that. It just proved what I knew already. Andrei was a creature of habit, and recent events had knocked him out of his comfort zone. He had been eager to reestablish his MO and stalk familiar prey. I wondered how many women who fit my description were on his list.

I could have gone up to Napa, but what was the use? It was pretty obvious who was responsible. He was long gone by now and back in his sanctuary. Billy's initial supposition could very well be true. But I didn't want to confront the fiend at the Ferry Building. Too many witnesses. Even at night there would be too many tourists, passersby, and indigents wandering around.

Maybe tracking him there and luring him to my kill zone would be the way to go. Even though he showed up in the damnedest places, I doubted my psychic connection to him. I'd never felt him or read his thoughts or anything trite and clichéd as that. But there had to be some kind of link. Maybe I was still too new to feel it.

I spent the next several nights searching the area in and around the Ferry Building, looking for Andrei's resting place. From Pier 1 to 14, I looked everywhere. I checked out the restaurants and shops and businesses. I investigated vestibules and elevator shafts. And there was one very frightened taco truck owner who was going to be telling his grandkids stories for years.

I had all but given up. Then it occurred to me that I had not actually gone inside the Ferry Building itself for some stupid reason. I searched it high and low. I checked all the restrooms and service closets. Nothing.

Then I noticed a pleasure boat docked nearby that hadn't been there before. It was sleek and black. Of course. It made perfect sense. This is how he was able to zip up and down the coast. He probably scooted right up the Napa River to get to Elektra. But how in the hell did he get over our innate fear of the water? Was it really that thing Julie had said? *"The car will carry you,"* or some such. Now it was a boat. So what was that bullshit about not being able to cross running water?

What really surprised me was the lack of security. No bodyguards, no sentries, no nothing. Arrogant bastard. Before long, I found my way below. I thought I would have to locate the cargo hold, but nope. Andrei's coffin was out in the open in the middle of a large compartment. It was exactly what you would expect from him. Black lacquer with what looked to be solid gold trim. The casket was open, and I could see the satin-lined interior. It was surrounded by thirteen candles on stands.

I hadn't brought my vampire exterminator kit with me, so I was not prepared to stay the night and end the fucker right then and there. I wanted to stick to my plan, although I didn't know when I would have a chance to execute it and him. My chance came sooner than later.

Just as I was getting ready to disembark from the boat, I saw Andrei coming up the gangplank. His eyes were cast down, so he didn't see me right away. I just stood there. When he did look up, genuine surprise lit his face up.

I waited until he got to the top of the ramp. We were almost nose to nose.

"Hello, asshole."

"Is that any way to greet ..."

"It is now. You are responsible for every lousy, disgusting, regrettable, deplorable thing that has happened to me the last two years. Remember what I said at Sarah's? You are going to pay for what you did to my brothers."

"Am I now? What makes you think that, little girl?"

I pulled my hand and arm back, and I slapped him across the face as hard as I could. The "smack" echoed off of the nearby buildings. He would never admit it, but the open-handed blow stung him, hurt him. It was insulting and painful. It had the intended effect. Before he could retaliate, I sprinted into a transformation and flew off, hoping he would follow and pursue me in fog or mist form. And that he did.

We both rode the wind. I led him to Mount Davidson, the highest point in San Francisco. I flew as fast as I could. I needed to give myself just a few extra seconds to transform. I flew southwest past Mission Dolores Park and through Noe Valley. I made sure the cloud of Andrei was still following me. I twisted and turned along the trails while the mist just flowed along methodically.

When I reached my destination I transformed into my "human" form. I located what I'd hoped would be here. Thankfully there were two of them. I destroyed one and turned a support post into a makeshift stake and hid it behind my back. I stood between my Andrei trap and the rolling fog.

Just as he got to within a few feet of me I screamed, "Come on, fucker!" His face started to materialize and ebb and flow with his gaseous form. I executed a backflip over the trap just as Andrei started to transform into a solid state. He solidified right into a net used to capture fog to make specialty vodka. Andrei's body and the mesh were one. And he was fucked.

"My dear maker, I thought of so many different ways I could have ended you. I was going to black bag you and truss you up the way you did me, but that wasn't good enough for you."

That night in Alameda, the billboard I saw? It was for vodka. Vodka made from San Francisco fog. The trick was getting him to one of the water capture sites. Damned if I didn't do just that.

"Let me go, Elizabeth! Set me free from this infernal fucking contraption!"

"Oh, Andrei, tsk, tsk. Come now. Such language." I was still hiding the stake behind my back.

"W-w-what are you going to do?"

"Isn't it obvious?"

"I gave you life, eternal life! You ungrateful bitch!"

"Ah, there's the rub, eh, Andrei? I never asked for it. And I sure as hell never asked for you."

I displayed the stake. I ran it from his neck down his chest to his stomach, popping buttons off his crisp, white dress shirt, exposing him. I laughed when I saw the intersection between mesh and flesh. He was visibly frightened.

"I-I-I'll do anything you ask. What is it you want? Money? Jewels?"

An evil cackle emanated from my throat as I tipped my head back and laughed.

"You really are a Eurotrash vampire cliché, aren't you? I

could stand here and detail all the ways you've wronged me, but that would give you too much time to weasel your way out of this predicament. I learned my lesson about playing with dead things."

"Elizabeth, please, wait ..." Numerous expressions contorted his face. Fear, anger, indignation. He shook violently, trying to free himself from my trap. He was caught between the physical and vapor. The net would not give way no matter how hard he struggled. The posts were secured, the net was strong, and he was done.

I raised my free hand and put my index finger to his lips. "Shhhhh. No more talking."

I looked around on the ground and found a good-sized rock. How convenient. I placed the point of the stake on his chest over his heart and drove it home with the stone. Andrei screamed. It was long and protracted, almost like he was faking it. Theatrical to the end. His eyes burned red. I struck the end of the post several times until the pointy end burst through his back. Black goo oozed from both wounds, and Andrei hung limply, gathered like so much fog water for $125-a-bottle vodka.

Saliva I couldn't muster but I still grabbed his hair, pulled his head up, and spit in his face just the same. It was symbolic and made me feel better.

"Fuck you."

Andrei solidified and was one with the net, which had woven its way through his body. There was no more movement. No lagoon for him to free himself from. No heavy chain around his neck to slough off. Huh. I wonder if it had been Jonas that saved his ass at Sutro Baths. Crazy idea when you think about it, since Jonas had been contracted by Ahura Mazda. But he had saved me how many times? I guess I would never know and at this point, I really didn't give a rat's ass.

CHAPTER XXVI

I screamed at the top of my lungs. It was a primal scream—a scream that I had waited to utter. It was victory, relief, and despair all rolled into one.

"I am Elizabeth Danae Rubis, and I am the Queen of the Fucking Night!"

This time it didn't take long for the thunder to clap and for the lightning to fork across and illuminate the sky. The rain came too, fast and hard. It was a downpour. I held my arms out and looked to the sky. The rainwater washed over me, cascading, washing grime and stress away. It pelted the patent leather and before long, pools and puddles filled along the trail I had taken to get to this spot.

That fresh rain smell filled the air. The petrichor was intoxicating.

I was thirsty as hell, and I opened my mouth. The water filled my maw, and I swallowed it, knowing full well that would not quench my thirst. But it eased the burning in my throat, if only for a moment. It would have to be expelled at some point, but that was another thing I didn't care about.

The rain dissipated, and the thunderclouds moved on as I calmed down. Ennui started to set in as I wiped the water from my face. I stood there for a long time looking at Andrei. It wasn't all that long ago that he had me crucified in a similar fashion. Once again, the irony was not lost on me.

This bastard had kidnapped me, murdered me, turned me into a vampire, killed my brothers and my sisters-in-law, and had had the nerve to tell me that I needed to check my feeding habits. On the other hand, he'd helped kill Da Rocha and dismantle what was left of the Order of Ahura Mazda. But I never had any affection for him, no affinity for him. Nothing but contempt and the desire for bloody revenge.

I never expected him to be a mentor or a teacher. The innate instincts that I'd acquired after the turning served me well. I knew to fear water and the sun. It was the fucking counting that I couldn't quite figure. I didn't have OCD when I was alive. Okay, maybe I was a bit anal, but never obsessive. Now, Jesus Christ, it was everything I could do to keep from counting shit. There were so many legends and so much mythology, I still didn't know or understand what was true and what wasn't. I knew what affected me and that was good enough for now. The electric blue eyes were another story.

Learning that I could still have sex was an exciting discovery, although I didn't quite understand these bisexual tendencies I had developed. Perhaps it was because I was uninhibited now. I wasn't going to let societal conventions and stereotypical gender and sex roles define my appetites. Not anymore. Why limit myself? Why not add all the pleasures of the flesh to my repertoire? What was to stop me? Morals? I was a murdering blood drinker with shape-shifting abilities. What the fuck did I care?

Adding sex to my kills was a twist I hadn't expected, but it was thrilling nonetheless. The prospect of using seduction as part of the hunt gave me all kinds of delicious ideas. But didn't I kind of start that way with the sales bros who wanted me for a ménage à trois? I just hadn't let it go that far.

Jonas really was par for the course. I shouldn't have been surprised that he betrayed me, considering my history with men. Whether it was the ones I chose to date or the ones my father picked for me, I never did find the one. Never Mr. Right, always Mr. Wrong. Now I could have Mr. Right Now. Or Miss. It was the way he'd betrayed me. I could almost understand if it had been a spur-of-the-moment thing and Ahura Mazda had him over a barrel. Extortion and black-mail were powerful tools.

But this was different.

He had played the long game with me. He had been in it for the long haul. Playing me, gaining my trust and confidence, and waiting for the right moment to strike. That moment in the cafe when he finally revealed himself to me boggled my mind. And what of his pals—the restaurateurs —were they in on it? Did they know what Jonas had been up to? Or did they just get caught in the crosshairs?

I guess it didn't really matter. They were dead now too. Speaking of counting, holy crap, I hadn't thought to try to come up with an accurate body count. Among me, Jonas, and Andrei—let alone Julie and Sarah—we had dispatched God knows how many people. I really didn't want to know. There was a handful that really mattered—my parents, Emily, Whitney, my brothers.

When the rain stopped I decided to take a stroll around Mount Davidson. After the stress of defeating Andrei had dissipated, I had a bounce in my step I hadn't known in a long time. I walked the paths along the edge. The dirt crunched under my boots as I walked. In all the years I'd lived here, in all of my now forty-six odd years of existence, I had never been here.

After taking in the views of San Francisco from high atop Mount Davidson, I found a shady spot and sat on the ground with my back against a tree. I was along the edge of a dirt trail. I knew I couldn't spend the rest of the night here. I needed to get to a sanctuary sooner than later. But a sense of accomplishment, that feeling of victory coursed through me, and I wasn't ready to call it a night.

I'd won.

My enemies were dead, vanquished. For all that I had endured, the things I had done, the things I had witnessed, the waves of SWAT cops, vampire slayers, and my own kind who would dispatch me or be my betters—I'd won. I'd survived. I'd endured. The morgue drawer couldn't hold me, the abandoned coal mine couldn't hold me, Jonas couldn't hold me, Andrei couldn't hold me, Tobias and his thugs couldn't hold me. Sarah couldn't hold me.

I had been smarter, stronger, and more resilient than any of those bastards.

Crossing my arms, I leaned back against the tree. I was feeling myself. I closed my eyes for a bit. I thought about what I would do next. A fresh start was what I needed, a new sanctuary, fresh hunting grounds. That old abandoned church was off limits. That had been Jonas's hideout once. Alcatraz wasn't the most convenient location, although the tourists were delivered daily. Sarah's house was an option. I could go back to the rail yard. The house at Moss Beach was enticing. It was good to know these places were available to me again, but I really did believe that I needed something new and different.

I'll sit here just a little while longer, I told myself. When I opened my eyes again I could have sworn I saw Blackfoot. She ran past me along the edge of the trail. How in the hell …?

I scrambled to my feet and chased after her. She wasn't running, but she wasn't exactly walking either. With me in tow, Blackfoot wound her way up toward the summit and took a trail I must have missed during my earlier meanderings. The path began to widen and curved slightly up ahead. That damned cat stayed just far enough ahead of me so I couldn't grab her.

I rounded the bend into a clearing, and I was blinded. The sun had begun to rise. I had lost all track of time, and I was up against it. Shielding my eyes, I tried to make out what was in front of me. A cross! A giant cross! It had to be a hundred feet tall. The sunlight seemed to pass directly through it. But it was really behind me and reflecting off this goddamned cross.

Falling to my knees, I screamed. "Oh, no, oh, God, no, no!" I threw my arms in front of my face, but the pain was unbearable. The light seared and burned my hands and whatever skin was exposed. I was on all fours, my head down, in a penitent position, but I was not going to repent. I was defiant.

It took every ounce of energy I could muster but I lifted my head and looked directly into the light reflecting off the concrete cross. It increased in intensity as the sun rose higher in the sky. My eyes radiated that electric blue light, I could see it in front of my face. Blackfoot came to me and rubbed and nuzzled my legs. What did she know? What the hell was she, really? Why had she led me to this spot? Did she really want me to die?

The blazing light got brighter and hotter. A large ball of fire formed in the middle of the cross and launched itself right at me and Blackfoot.

"Well, fuck."

- The End -

ACKNOWLEDGMENTS

The author would like to thank ...

My family of course, without their support, these stories would stay in my head eating away at my synapses and that wouldn't be good for anyone. My wife has allowed me to walk around in another woman's skin for the better part of three years now ... the numerous people (and hopefully now new readers) who have stopped by to chat, buy a book or take a postcard at my book signing events ... everyone who has taken the time to write a review — your feedback means more than you could possibly know ... Trifecta Publishing House — Lori, Doug and Diana ... the inimitable Jodi McDermitt, who continues to encourage my ramblings ... numerous cousins, friends, colleagues and co-workers who also encourage these endeavors and ask incessantly, "When is the next book coming out?"

And that truly is the $64,000 question, isn't it?

ABOUT THE AUTHOR

Jerry Knaak, a 10-year U.S. Navy veteran, has been writing professionally in one form or another for more than 25 years.

A native of Rochester, N.Y., he enlisted in the Navy upon graduation from Edison Tech in 1987. Since serving as a radio and television personality in with Armed Forces Radio and Television at Naval Air Station Keflavik, Iceland, and as a writer for *Naval Aviation News* magazine in Washington, D.C., Jerry has worked with the Oakland Raiders professional football team for the past 18 years. He has produced thousands of articles for online publication during his career. After 16 years in digital media, he is now serving as the team historian. Knaak started his sports writing career with *Baltimore Football Weekly*, covering the Baltimore Stallions of the Canadian Football League.

Jerry currently lives in Northern California with his wife Angi and youngest son Noah, three cats, a dog, numerous koi fish, and any number of vagrant spiders and lizards. His oldest son, William, is attending college in Florida.

When he's not writing gritty tales of terror or researching gridiron heroics, Jerry enjoys reading, watching movies and good serial television. He is also an avid blogger and hosts a regular podcast.

The Dark Terror is his third novel.

Printed in April 2019
by Rotomail Italia S.p.A., Vignate (MI) - Italy